VENGEFUL

Severinov Bratva: Book Three

KRISTEN LUCIANI

Vengeful © 2019 by Kristen Luciani

This book is a work of fiction. Names, characters, places and incidents are the product of the author's imagination or are used fictitiously. Any resemblance to actual events, locales or persons, living or dead is purely coincidental.

Except for the original material written by the author, all songs, song titles, and lyrics mentioned in this novel are the property of the respective songwriters and copyright holders.

All rights reserved. The unauthorized reproduction or distribution of this copyrighted work is illegal. This book or any portion thereof may not be reproduced, scanned, distributed, or used in any manner whatsoever, via the Internet, electronic, or print, without the express written permission of the author, except for the use of brief quotations in a book review.

For more information, or information regarding subsidiary rights, please contact Kristen Luciani at kluciani@gmail.com

Edited by: Elaine York of Allusion Graphics

Cover Design by: Cosmic Letterz

❧ Created with Vellum

PROLOGUE

Cristian

"*Daddy's dead.*"

I let out a deep sigh, pressing my fingertips to my temples as I stare up at the early morning sky. The horizon is smeared with streaks of gold, orange, and yellow, the sun just poking above the clouds. Aside from the haunting memory of my sister Gianna's tearful voice, the only other sound that consumes my conscious is the crashing surf on the shore of Plage des Fourmis Beach in Monaco.

It's been six weeks, and I berate myself every day for not being able to stop the attack.

I should have been there with them.

I could have saved him.

But my father was on borrowed time, and in this life, it doesn't take long for the other shoe to drop. There are too many enemies lurking in the shadows, poised to attack in the name of jealousy, power, and revenge.

And years back, when my grieving father opened the fucking door and invited the enemy in for espresso and cannoli, I knew

I'd eventually be the one to grab the reins and make sure the rest of my family didn't suffer the same fate.

It was only a matter of time before I'd have to step into position, avenge his murder, and secure the livelihood of the Marcone name.

I just never expected that our lives would ultimately be shattered by our own blood.

White-capped crests gather speed and force as they crash over the sand, and I draw in a deep breath, letting the salty sea air fill my lungs.

It's calm here. Peaceful. So different from what I'm used to back home in Sicily where danger looms on a daily basis.

A place where death isn't a fear, it's a reality.

And a definite possibility when your family has commanded control of all sea ports spanning the entire coastline of Europe and most of Asia. And we're talking hostile takeover shit. Our shipping company didn't grow to become the largest in the world because my father was a savvy businessman who understood contracts and legalities and regulations.

He only knew his own brand of ruthless negotiation.

It's either mine...

Or it's mine.

It was like an iron fist, one that would come crashing down on the head of anyone who dared oppose him or worse, decline an offer to 'work with him.'

I grit my teeth.

And my family calls *me* the loose cannon.

I guess the grape doesn't fall far from the vine.

I drag myself to my feet, my sneakers making deep indentations in the packed sand as I lunge from side to side, stretching out my quads. Running along the shore of the Mediterranean is the closest I come to the water.

I never let it touch me, not since it almost sucked the life out of me when I was younger.

But yet, it's the one place where I feel the most at peace.

And in my line of work, since peace usually accompanies death, it's damn poetic.

I slip my AirPods into my ears, pushing my sunglasses farther up my nose and pulling the brim of my baseball cap down low over my face.

Because you just never know who's watching.

The same people who targeted Dad and his hot-headed business partner, Daniel Tava, are coming for the rest of us. That's how it works with Cosa Nostra. You eliminate the enemy and then you incinerate everything that they leave behind.

And everyone.

That's why my brother Diego and I came to Monaco posing as hoteliers. After Tava was killed here in a suspicious hit-and-run, we knew the enemy was closing in fast, itching to take over everything he and my father built.

Our only option is to find them before they find us.

I turn up the volume of my music and take off like a thoroughbred out of the gate, as if I can evade the threat of demise that's been hot on my heels for as long as I can remember.

It would be nice, but completely and utterly impossible at the same time.

I let the angry lyrics of the song blaring in my ears mute the toxic thoughts exploding between my temples like bullets.

My feet pound the sand, my calf muscles tight with every step I take. Sand kicks up all around me, gritty against my damp skin, but it only drives me harder.

I pick up speed, my legs pumping faster and faster. Running helps me escape, if only from myself. My breaths are short and sharp, in through my nose, out through my mouth. Rage builds deep inside of me, coursing through my veins as I push myself forward. Wind whips around me, and for a fleeting second, I'm free of it all.

Sweat drizzles down the side of my face, my chest and back pebbled with perspiration. I pull off my cap to swipe at my forehead, knocking out an AirPod. I grunt, lunging forward to grab it before it hits the sand. My hand juts out, the little white earpiece slipping right through my damn fingers as a crushing force takes my body airborne for what seems like hours before my back crashes onto the sand with a hard thud.

And I only have a split second to choke out a yelp before something lands on top of me.

Something slick.

Something smooth.

Something that suddenly has my cock rock-hard beneath these flimsy Under Armour shorts.

I open my eyes a crack, squinting in the sun since my sunglasses flew off my face mid-flight. Piercing blue eyes narrow at me, full pink lips twisted into a grimace, tanned skin flushed and glowing.

"What the hell are you doing here?" My assailant hisses, her teeth clenched. "This is private property!"

I force my eyes away from her perfect tits, the ones bulging out of her sports bra and pressed tight against me. "What did you say?"

"I said," she seethes. "You shouldn't be here. This beach belongs to *me*."

I grin as her face becomes more and more pinched. "I don't see any names written on the sand."

"This beach is part of my resort." She glares at me, her chest heaving, hands still pressed into the sand, flanking me on both sides.

Interesting. I didn't expect my 'competition,' the owner of the hotel next door, to be female, much less have a porn star body and the tongue of a viper.

"Then your resort must be in pretty bad shape since there isn't a single person out here other than us. Maybe you need to work on your people skills." I smirk as her nostrils flare. There's fire raging deep in this woman, and I don't think I'm gonna need to press too many more buttons before it unleashes all over me.

And that *really* has my cock twitching.

She gasps and recoils. "Are you seriously—?"

I nod, bringing myself onto my elbows. "I'm a guy, and you're half-naked. *And* sweaty." I flash a mischievous smile. "I only have so much self-control, sweetheart."

"You're a disgusting pig!"

"And yet, you're still on top of me." I fold my arms behind my head. "Don't get me wrong. I'm not complaining. In fact, I'm happy to stay here all day long and let you yell at me, as long as you don't get dressed."

Her eyes widen and she lets out a gasp that makes me think she'd pummel me with a piece of driftwood if there was one within reach.

Thank fuck there isn't.

She leans back on her heels, still straddling me. "You're trespassing," she says in a terse voice. "If you don't leave now..."

"What? You're gonna have me arrested? Do you really want to do that? Because it doesn't look like you're that eager to get away from me right now. Admit it. You like what you see."

"What I see is an arrogant asshole with no regard for rules *or* decency." Her eyes blaze with anger, sparks flying from the depths and singeing my skin. Desire courses through me, my palms itching to slide over the luscious curves of her hips and ass.

"I have complete regard for decency. If I didn't, I'd have already told you to switch positions with me."

Her mouth drops open, and I let out a chuckle. "Not into that, huh?"

"I have a boyfriend," she rasps.

I lean up on my elbows, drawing myself up toward her. "So you have a boyfriend, and you're still here, sitting on top of me, a half-naked and clearly aroused stranger. Tell me, gorgeous. Is he the one you're running from?"

The woman lets out a choked cry as she loses her balance and tumbles backward, her long blonde ponytail whipping against her shoulder.

"Looks like I struck a nerve," I say. "Are you trying to escape from what you settled for because you're afraid that you can't find something better?"

"Who the hell are you to analyze me like that?"

This part is gonna be fun.

"I just figured we should get to know each other a little better, now that I've taken over Villa d'Este." My lips curl upward as the shocked expression settles into her features. "I'm your new neighbor, Cristian Marcone."

Chapter One
TALI

TWO WEEKS LATER

Chaos.

Pure and utter chaos.

It's hovered over me like a dark ominous cloud for my entire life, so is it any real surprise that it followed me here to Monaco, a place that was supposed to bring me peace and comfort in the wake of Dad's death?

He's gone, but evidently, his legacy lives on.

Tall glass windows lining the front of my hotel shatter from the deafening blast, shades of orange and yellow bursting into the air. Tears sting my eyes, not from the fumes but from the horrific memories forever etched into my mind. I've heard these sounds before, seen this devastation.

No, I can't focus on that now.

The ground rumbles beneath our feet as we run right into the mass hysteria. My throat is tight, a gaggle of tears damn near choking me as my sandals slap against the pavement.

Only seconds earlier, I'd been standing at the shore of Plage des Fourmis with my brothers and my boyfriend Alain, mourning my father.

Only seconds earlier I'd been silently berating myself for the millionth time about why I wasn't there to help him, why I couldn't do anything to stop yet another tragedy from pummeling my family.

I had one chance to prevent it from happening, and I blew it.

We lost so much that day, and it was my fault.

I'll never forgive myself for the mistakes I made, the ones that changed our family unit forever. I will regret them until the day I die.

Dammit, I could have done something to stop it!

I was prepared!

Because Dad taught me that.

But today?

Screams pierce the air, shards of glass and metal flying in all directions. I tackle a middle-aged couple nearby and push them to the ground to get them out of the line of fire.

Today, I forgot everything he taught me. I succumbed to the grief and lost sight of everything else.

And I was definitely not prepared for the mayhem that was just unleashed at my posh, beachside resort.

"Tali!"

I look up to find my brothers running toward the resort. Their faces are pinched with worry and panic. If Alain and I had walked up the beach a minute earlier, things would have been very different...for me *and* for them.

Speaking of Alain...I crane my neck, my heart thumping hard in my chest. Oh my God, where did he—?

A peripheral glance confirms that he's down on the ground several feet away.

By himself.

I roll my eyes.

What a selfish and self-absorbed jerk.

I hate that I let Alain Leclercq suck me into his toxic funnel cloud. Now I'm just spiraling, worse than I was before I got involved with him in the first place.

If circumstances were different, I'd have already dumped his pompous ass. Unfortunately, I learned my very harsh lesson much too late.

I lift my head slightly, waving my hand in the air, letting my brothers know I'm okay.

Physically, at least.

Mentally, though? I'm a hot mess.

Kaz and Leo run over to me, diving to the ground next to me. "Christ, Tali! What the hell happened?" Kaz demands, pulling me in for a hug.

"Are you hurt?" Leo asks.

"No," I whisper, then let out a gasp. "Oh my God! Where's Myla?" Myla is Leo's wife and she'd been with us on the beach, too.

"She's fine. I told her to stay down on the shore."

"As if I'd listen to you," a female voice quips, approaching from behind and kneeling down next to us.

I throw my arms around her. "You're really not great at that listening thing, you know? We need to work on it."

She shrugs and squeezes my hand. "My family needed me. You can't edge me out that easily."

I hold the side of my head, which I scraped when I crashed to the pavement. "What the hell happened?" I groan, looking at the streaks of blood on my hand. "All of these people...holy shit, they're freaking the fuck out!" My voice cracks, and I swallow a sob. Jesus, not now. I cannot do this now!

I'm in charge here. Me, nobody else. I need to take control of this shit storm and fix it!

"I have no goddamn clue what's going on," Kaz says, jumping to his feet. "Someone must have seen something, though. T, we need to clear this place out. You know, just in case."

Yeah, just in case whoever bombed my hotel decides they didn't do enough damage the first time and wants to give it another go.

"Where's—?" Kaz looks around and groans. "For fuck's sake, Leclercq! Always busy covering your own ass, huh? Did you even think of my sister's ass?" He calls out to Alain with a roll of his eyes. "Wait, forget I asked that question."

"Fuck off, Kaz. What was I supposed to do, run into the goddamn fire?" Alain scoffs.

"Kaz, don't start." I mutter. "I'm not in the mood, and there are more important things to handle."

"He's still a cocksucker," he mutters, pulling me to my feet. "Come on, we need answers." We walk around the decimated lobby, sidestepping people running from the building. Sirens blare out in the distance, and Kaz grips my hand tighter. "Don't think about it, Tali," he hisses to me. "Don't let it get you again."

I try. God, I try so damn hard. But the shrieks and cries and the noxious smell of smoke and chemicals make my stomach clench and a sob catches in my throat. I swallow it down, praying that it stays buried, just like everything else threatening to bubble over.

I've been here before.

But Kaz is right.

I can't let myself go back.

The valets are trying to keep some kind of order as guests spill out of the hotel dragging their luggage, demanding their cars. Security surrounds the perimeter, guns drawn.

Just in case.

My catch phrase.

I scan the crowd, my temples pounding from the noise erupting around me. I wave at Sasha, my head of security, but he doesn't see me. I push through the crowd with Kaz on my heels. "Sasha!" I yell. He looks up and shakes his head.

A lump forms in my throat, my eyes burning from the smoke billowing around him. Oh my God, why is he shaking his head at me? Is somebody dead? Did they find another bomb? Holy shit! Is this happening? Has my hotel really been attacked?

I finally reach a small clearing where Sasha is standing and gasp.

I can finally see why he's by himself.

Flames engulf what looks like a luggage trunk. From the bits of it that scatter over the pavers in the hotel driveway, I can tell it's Louis Vuitton.

A luxury bomb casing.

How original.

But that's not what makes my heart thump and pound harder with each passing second.

It's the car next to the flame-engulfed trunk.

The bright orange Ferrari Portofino.

Well, at least it *was* orange.

Now it's charred black on one side...the side closest to the remains of the trunk.

The passenger side.

The metal has been folded in like an accordion from the impact of the blast, all of the windows shattered. Shards of glass glitter on the pavement surrounding the car, which is still engulfed in flames.

"Sasha," I whisper, the lump growing to the point where it's almost impossible to draw in a single breath. "That's—"

The sirens get louder and police cars and fire trucks swarm the vicinity before I can even blink. The police force in Monaco is the largest in the world, considering that the number of officers employed have such a small area to cover. So first responders are pretty much immediate responders.

Thank God for that.

A group of firefighters jump off their trucks and immediately go to work on putting out the flames. Cops jump out of their cars, armed with weapons and explosive-sniffing dogs. They storm the hotel, securing the perimeter, including the beach behind us. Whoever did this won't get away. Not on their watch.

"Jesus Christ," Kaz mutters. But even as he stares at the smoking rubble, the reality evades him.

But it hits me like a baseball bat to the side of the head, and I can't ignore it anymore.

This was a targeted attack.

A chill settles deep in my bones as I stare at the smoking car.

I leave Kaz with Sasha and I keep moving, slithering through the crowds to get to the person in charge. "Excuse me," I huff, finally pushing through the last group of rubberneckers. Jesus, don't they want to take cover?

You know, *just in case?*

The officer looks at me with a stone-cold glare but says nothing.

My lips stretch into a tight line. "I'm the owner of this hotel. Natalya Severinov."

"Looks like you've had a bit of trouble here, Ms. Severinov," he says in a sarcastic tone.

"You think?" I narrow my eyes. "Listen, I want to cooperate with you and your team. Tell me what needs to be done. I want to make sure my guests are safe and protected, and the rest of the hotel needs to be evacuated and checked for—"

"Let's start with the basics. Where were you when the blast went off?"

I recoil. Um, relevance? Shouldn't we be working together to find the bastard who did this instead of rehashing my schedule? "I was on the beach with my family. I came back toward the hotel, and when I was next to the golf course, I heard the blast."

"And why were you on the beach instead of being here at the hotel?" He cocks an eyebrow and I swallow a gasp. Is he implying something...that I *knew* it was going to happen?

"Look," I seethe, waving my hands around me. "There are a lot of innocent people here who are confused and scared and upset, and there may still be a psycho running around here, looking for the next target! We need to do something other than talk about why I was on the beach today!" My voice rises, cracking, and I know the tears are close.

Argh! I need to shut this down now!

Forget what I've seen, what I know!

I clutch the sides of my head, struggling to keep calm. "I have a duty to protect these people." I hear myself say it, but deep down, I know the 'people' are not the ones at risk.

The evidence pretty much confirms that.

A hand clamps down on my shoulder and a deep voice from behind almost immediately soothes me.

"Officer," my brother Alek says. "I spoke to the head valet, and he has some information you might find useful." He nods over to the group of drivers being bombarded by bomb-sniffing dogs and their owners.

The officer nods and gives me a final critical look before walking into the mayhem. The flames are out, but the devastation remains.

So do the unanswered questions of who and why.

God only knows, there are plenty of potential answers.

Enemies are never few in number. Not for people like us.

People who have dark secrets that match their dark lives.

Someone always has a way of unearthing them.

And the price of keeping them quiet is never cheap.

My shoulders quake under Alek's firm grip. I look around at the police barricading people from the hotel. One after another, they run into the front entrance with their explosive kits and hounds. I can't breathe, and it's not from the smoke inhalation.

What festers inside of me makes my chest tight. A sharp pain assaults my heart. This is not the time to think about what could have been. Or what *should* have been.

But there are people who don't want me to forget it.

I've been waiting for this day.

I knew it would eventually come.

I'm just not prepared.

Fuck! I'm not prepared!

I clutch the sides of my head, avoiding my brother's eyes. This is one thing I can't bring myself to tell him.

I made my bed, thought I was doing the right thing for the family.

They fucked me really good.

Convinced me it was my only option.

My eyes flood with tears.

No, telling Alek would mean an all-out war, and I can't lose my brothers. They're all I have left.

I suck in a few breaths, trying to silence the demons, at least until I can make sense of this. I need help, but the only person I can turn to is the one who put me in the middle of this shit show in the first place.

"Tali," Alek murmurs. "You need to get your shit together. You look like you're going to crumble. You're the boss here. Reel it in and control this mess!"

I nod quickly, my teeth chattering despite the intense afternoon heat. I watch his lips move as he directs me to do this, that, and the other. But I don't hear a word he says. I'm too busy trying to keep the panic from bubbling over and consuming me as I stand in front of my hotel.

Girl boss, girl boss, girl boss.

I am a fucking boss!

When the hell did I become such a goddamn basket case?

I fist my hair.

I take that back. I know exactly when it happened.

Daddy, Daddy, Daddy...I miss you so much...

I should have been there for you.

I could have helped.

I could have saved you!

I release a shaky breath. If Dad had been around, maybe things would be—

No! I am not playing that game! I made that decision as part of my role in this family, and now I have to live with it.

And whatever repercussions come along with it.

This time, only a car was decimated.

I need to be ready for the next time...so that I'm not the one in the path of destruction.

There is no other option.

I have to be prepared.

"Are you even on this planet with me right now, Tali?" Alek snaps a finger in front of my face. "Did you hear a goddamn word I just said?"

"Yes," I rasp. "I got it. We need to...to..." Crap. I really have no freaking clue what he just said.

He rolls his eyes. "Jesus Christ," he mumbles. "You're the owner here. You need to take control of this! The paparazzi are already all over the damn place. They're looking for you. And if they see you like this...like a fucking hot mess who can't even speak," he shakes his head. "Well, that bomb may as well have leveled the place. It'll be over, Tali. You need to make them see you have things under control, that shit like this won't be tolerated. That you won't be a victim!"

If only he knew.

I already am.

And I deserve it.

I got their message loud and clear.

But it won't be the last.

I swipe my fingers under my eyes in a futile attempt to make myself look human, although I'm pretty sure my eyeliner is smudged beyond repair right now.

An obnoxiously loud sound roars behind us, and I roll my eyes. Here we go with the tabloid photogs.

They love this shit. Scandals and slayings. It's what their readers crave.

Everyone wants a glimpse into the underworld.

Lucky for them, they can escape it without fear of being sucked in.

I, on the other hand, am sinking deeper into the murk with each passing day.

There's no way out for me.

There's just darkness.

And looming danger.

Chapter Two
TALI

I run a hand through my hair and smooth the front of my sheath dress. "I will get this mess under control. Don't worry."

"What you've *got* is hundreds of people looking for another place to stay since yours seems to be a little too well done for their taste."

I clench my fists, twisting in the direction of the arrogant and deliciously infuriating voice. Cristian Marcone. How utterly inconvenient. "Was this your pathetic ploy to get more guests fleeing to your shithole hotel, Cristian? Are you here to poach my guests?"

He stares at me with those deep, dark eyes...ones I've regrettably allowed myself to fantasize about ever since I barreled into him that day on the beach. And I hate myself more and more each time I think about the cuts of muscle on his chest that I long to trace with my fingers.

And my tongue...

"Sloppy seconds? Not a chance. We have standards at the Villa d'Este. You take in a very different crowd, Tali." He smirks. "I don't think they'd be comfortable in our villas. Or paying our rates, for that matter." He looks around. "This is more of an economy hotel, yes?"

Argh! I detest myself!

My eyes widen so much that they are about to pop out of my damn head. The fucking nerve. God, do I want to punch that smug-ass grin off his perfectly chiseled face! "First, call me Natalya," I seethe. "Only my friends call me Tali. And *you* are no friend of mine, Marcone."

He cocks a thick, dark eyebrow. "And second? Please tell me there's more. Come on, don't leave me hanging."

I push myself toward him, not that he flinches even the slightest bit. "Second, this is one of the most exclusive properties in Monaco. I have every racer for the Formula One Grand Prix on my guest list!"

Alek clears his throat. "Not every one."

I turn to him, my nostrils flaring and my fists itching at my sides. "Thanks, great timing, as usual."

My brother nods, his usual stoic expression intact. "Anytime."

"If it isn't the man, the myth, and the legend." Cristian grins at Alek, clapping him on the back. "You've been holed up at the top of the mountain lately. What brought you down? The threat of a hostile takeover?"

Alek smirks. "Not if you're the guy running it. I wouldn't lose a fucking wink of sleep over that."

"Wow, it's really not my day, huh? And here I was, just stopping by to see if you needed some help since it looks like your 'exclusive property' is under siege." His eyes rake over the length of my body, launching a delicious assault on every single nerve ending.

Damn him.

I hate him.

I want him.

I am officially head case central.

"Tali! What the fuck is going on here?" And there's a voice that has pretty much the opposite effect of Cristian's on me. It's arrogant, it's infuriating.

But it owns me.

Motherfucker.

I swallow the agitation before it sends me plunging off the deep end once again. "Alain," I say, trying to mask the disdain from my voice.

It doesn't really work, but then again, he doesn't seem to notice.

Or care.

"Is that my fucking car?" He yells, pushing back his hair. His green eyes are wild, his expression full of rage. "What in the hell happened? *What?*" He screams before shoving his way through the crowd toward his smoking hot car.

About twenty minutes ago, it was an entirely different kind of smoking hot car.

Kaz's hearty chuckle resonates behind us. "Looks like LePrick's ride was the biggest fatality of the day. When we figure out who did this, I'm gonna shake the motherfucker's hand before plugging the asshole." He turns his ice-blue gaze toward Cristian. "Who the hell are you?"

Cristian's eyes narrow as he and Kaz size each other up.

Christ. There is way too much testosterone flooding these guys right now.

"Kaz, this is Cristian Marcone, owner of Villa d'Este," I say, craning my neck to see where my 'boyfriend' went. Only seconds earlier, he was chewing out one of the cops. Now he's gone.

I'd like to say it's for good.

I'd like to say I'm that lucky.

Judging from the looks of that car, I guess maybe I am. For the time being, at least.

But Leclercq? He's not going anywhere.

He's already made that pretty damn clear.

"Marcone, huh?" Kaz nods and looks at me. "So this is the dickhead you talk about all the time?"

"All the time, huh?" Cristian winks at me and folds his arms. "Nice."

"Didn't you just hear the word dickhead in the same sentence?" I snip.

"Yeah, but that doesn't bother me. I know I'm an acquired taste."

"Which I have no desire to sample," I fume, trying desperately to squelch the sensations coursing through me. Every cell is on high alert, his spicy scent teasing my flared nostrils.

Cristian's low, husky chuckle makes my knees wobble, and in these heels, that's not a good thing.

This guy turns me on like a light switch every time he's near.

He makes me forget.

I like that.

I like *him*.

But I know I can't have him.

Leclercq has me shackled to him, and he's thrown away the key.

Only one thing can set me free.

The all-out war.

Either way, I lose.

This way keeps the people I love safe.

I had my chance.

I wasted it.

Now I'm paying the price.

I clear my throat, hating like hell that my brothers are exchanging a very amused look right now.

I can see the curiosity. I can sense the inquisition.

Five, four, three...

"You think your boyfriend is gonna sue you for the damages to his precious car, T?" Kaz quips, throwing an arm around my shoulder.

I shake him off, my eyes darting to Cristian's deflated expression. But it doesn't take long for it to shift back to his signature cocky asshole façade.

"Boyfriend, huh?" he asks, although it's not really a question, thanks to my big-mouthed, twin brother.

"Yeah," I mutter, shooting a death glare in Kaz's direction.

"You know, this whole thing doesn't really seem like a big mystery to me anymore. I mean, it's pretty fucking obvious that the person who did this was trying to make the air here a little less toxic by taking out that frog." Kaz winks at me and grabs Alek, pulling him away from us. "We'll do damage control. You stay here and make sure your guests don't follow the Pied Piper back to his hotel." He snickers, nodding at Cristian.

"Your brothers don't seem worried about what happened." Cristian's eyebrows knit together. "Why?"

I rub my hands up and down my pebbled skin. Goosebumps. In eighty-degree sunshine. All because of him.

"Alek never shows his hand. The wheels are turning, but he never lets you see what's happening behind the scenes." I sigh. "And Kaz…he's the comic. The loose cannon. He's trying to make me feel better about things, but behind his jokes, he's always plotting."

"So things with your family aren't what they seem?"

"Never." I stare into his chocolate-brown gaze. "And how about yours?"

He flashes a half-smile. "Every family has their own secrets and skeletons."

"I'm sure yours has more than most, considering it owns practically all of Sicily."

"I'll bet you've got plenty of your own," he murmurs, so close that I can feel the whisper of his breath on my cheek.

I swallow hard. "Is that why you're here? To see if I'll share something that you can take advantage of?" My lips stretch into a tight line. "Guess again. You're not going to make this into something you can use against me. So why don't you just get back onto your little moped and ride off a cliff, Marcone?"

He grins, his bright white smile blinding me for a brief second. Good God, doesn't he have a single flaw? Even the scar above his right eyebrow looks like it was meant to exist there. It makes him no less perfect. No less delectable.

But damn, it does make him sexier. And much more dangerous.

Cristian scrubs a hand down the front of his stubble-peppered face, and I bite down hard on my lip, wondering how it would feel to have his face pressed against mine, to taste his lips on my own.

He closes the distance between us, dipping his head lower so that our foreheads almost touch. "That's one thing I've learned over the years, Natalya. I don't need to look for things to use against my enemies. They usually look for *me*."

Chapter Three
CRISTIAN

The sun dips lower, making the clouds in front of it glow brightly. Orange, red, and blue streaks light up the horizon as I weave around curves, taking sharp turns on my Triumph Bonneville Speedmaster. I take long deep breaths, drinking in the sea air as the wind whips through me.

I need this.

It's my release, my own personal form of therapy.

I don't need to spill out my problems to some shrink on a couch.

No, I just need to take out my bike and ride until my mind is clear.

Christ only knows I do enough every day to muck it up.

There are more cars on the road right now. More people, too.

The place is crawling with A-listers from all over the world, here for the Formula One Grand Prix.

It's one of the biggest spectator events of the year, and the only reason why my next stop is local.

Otherwise, I'd have had to take a little weekend trip to Rome to find him.

But lucky me, he's here for the race. So are his cronies, but I'll deal with them when the time comes.

Right now, Giovanni Viva is my target.

He's been marked for playing a very dangerous game.

A game others are playing just as hard.

Right now, there are no clear winners. But I'll be taking care of that soon enough.

He thinks he got away with it. He thinks we don't know what he did, what he *took*.

Which is the only reason he'd ever invite me to his chalet.

Fucking idiot.

But he took too much this time.

He's stolen what can never be returned.

What can never be replaced.

So keep taking, motherfucker. Keep trying to outsmart one of the biggest organizations in the world. People think just because the head is cut off, the rest of the body writhes until it's put to sleep for good.

Not so with this organization.

Our organization.

The one I call my family.

We've only become stronger without the head.

And the world is about to find out just how strong we actually are.

I park my bike along the side of a heavily traveled road along the shore where restaurants and bars line each side. I pull off my helmet, run my fingers through my hair, and take a quick look around. High-powered, heavily bankrolled drunks as far as the eye can see. Millionaires and billionaires. Ignorant as the day is long.

That's their bliss.

Unfortunately for the millionaire I'll soon be visiting, ignorance represents something very different.

There is a narrow footpath leading up a steep hill toward a chalet. I've been up there a few times. It's nestled deep into the trees, impossible to spot from the road. Even the power players take to hiding. They jump into their caves where they lurk and wait for an opportunity to seize a long-awaited prize, trying not to get killed in the process.

The dipshit invited me anyway. He still doesn't realize what I know, what I've known for weeks, and what's going to be his downfall.

And loyalty doesn't mean dick without a hefty fee attached to it.

A few minutes later, I rap on the front door with the heavy brass knocker, and Gio greets me with a big smile.

"Cristian!" he bellows, pulling me in for a hug and kissing me on both cheeks.

As if the fact that I'm his nephew means a goddamn thing when he's already stabbed me in the back one time too many.

It's because of him that my father is lying in a wooden box right now, six feet under.

Greedy bastard.

It's time to pay up.

"Uncle," I say, walking into the chalet.

"I saw the hotel. We drove by when we arrived yesterday," Uncle Gio says with an appraising smile. He pours me a glass of chianti, handing it to me. "There are others, yes? Doing the same type of business?"

"Many others," I say, sipping the ruby red liquid. "And yes, they are doing well. Very well. We have a unique clientele with special needs that only we can accommodate. Makes for a profitable niche."

"It also makes you very powerful," Gio says, nodding his approval. He's practically salivating at the idea of owning a piece of what we've built.

But I don't make deals with scumbags.

And he's underestimated me once too often.

"It does," I say. Something you really should have remembered before you invited me here, Uncle.

"And my brother-in-law, rest his soul, he was your partner in the hotel business, yes?"

Moving in for the kill early. He must have a hot date tonight.

I almost choke on my next words because the lack of remorse in his voice makes me sick. But I play because it's the only way to win this hand.

"He was. I don't have to tell you how hard it's been on all of us with Dad being gone…" I shake my head. My asshole uncle didn't even make it to the fucking funeral. Maybe that was because he was too busy trying to figure out how he was going to take control of our livelihood once the boss was out of the picture.

"I know, and that's why I invited you up here. I wanted to see how I could help your family. Tell me," he says, his oversized body sinking into a couch cushion. "What do you plan to do with the shipping business down in Sicily? You can't possibly manage it on your own, being here in Monaco with your hotel. And Diego..." Gio smirks and sips his wine. "He's not exactly the one with the killer business instinct, is he?"

That I can't argue. My brother Diego is happiest and most productive when he's balls-deep in hot European models. That's where he does his best work.

But like any good businessman, Diego also knows that pussy can be exchanged for information. So while he's a notorious playboy who likes to bang women three at a time, he also knows when and how to use them for his own financial gain.

And if Gio was any bit as enterprising as my deviant brother, he'd already know why I'm really here in Monaco.

To find my father's killer.

I down the rest of my wine, the smooth liquid sliding down my throat.

Gio refills my glass. I guess he thinks I'll get all loose-lipped if I'm drunk.

Not a shot, Uncle.

I stare at him and wait for what I know is coming next.

He twists his hands together and takes a long drink. "I could help you expand, Cristian. I have connections who are willing to pay a lot of money for access to our ports."

Our ports? Is he fucking kidding me?

"I don't know if I'm ready to break up our shipping business yet. It's too soon to think about that." I avert my eyes, trying hard to look like the guy whose dad was gunned down at a farm stand without a single witness or lead on the identification of the murderer.

Oh, right.

I don't have to pretend.

"You don't want to wait, Cristian," my uncle says in a tone bordering on desperation. "It's been two months since your father died. If too much more time passes, our enemies will take it over. They will seize our territories. They will bury our family! We will lose everything!"

"*We* will?"

Uncle Gio clears his throat. "Well, uh, yes, of course. We are blood! I take this loss as hard as you do, nephew. I want to find the people who did this and make them pay! But the most important thing for us to do right now is to band together in a show of strength. Let me run things for you and the others. You are grieving now, not thinking straight. I can bring in my men and make sure we remain a force of strength in those areas! There is too much at risk, too much money to be claimed. Your mother, my sister, would want it that way."

My mouth twists at the mention of my mother who passed away years ago from breast cancer. I clench my fists, ready to launch them at his fat fucking face. I'd like nothing more than to split his head open right here and now.

"Tommy, Vince, and Anthony are handling things back home," I say in a flat voice, referring to my other brothers.

"And Gianna? She must need help, too."

My sister Gianna is more lethal than all of us put together. In fact, I had to talk her off the ledge when she found out I was making the visit to Uncle Gio. She'd been planning to skin him alive herself, but I told her to hold off, that she should save her strength for the bastard who actually pulled the trigger.

That's what happens when you grow up as the only girl in a family full of testosterone-driven men. You learn how to take care of yourself and everyone who so much as looks at you cross-eyed.

And believe me, she did the time.

"Everyone is managing. Nobody wants to let the business go." I study my uncle, narrowing my eyes at him. His gaze falls to the floor where his foot taps fast and furious against the polished hardwood floor. My eyes flicker left and right as the hint of a cool breeze floats into the room. I breathe in, a sudden musky scent assaulting my nostrils.

My uncle only reeks of provolone, a smell hardly comparable to an expensive cologne.

The hairs on the back of my neck prickle.

Adrenaline courses through my veins, my fingers gripping the arm of the couch.

Just a little bit closer.

Just...

A...

Little...

Bit.

Uncle Gio stands suddenly, backing away from the couch and knocking into the coffee table. The bottle of chianti overturns, the red liquid drizzling onto the floor. It stains the wood a deep, dark red.

Just like the color of blood.

And it sure as fuck won't be mine.

I swivel around when I hear the flick of a wrist behind me. A big beefy guy has a piece of wire wrapped between his two fingers, trying to choke me with it. I duck and swerve, flipping him over my shoulder so that his body crashes through the table.

Split in two.

Exactly what I want to do to my bastard of an uncle.

In good time.

I pound the face of the guy a few times who's moaning on the floor and my body is yanked backward by my hair. Another guy drags me across the floor toward the kitchen. I dig my heels into the grooves of the wood, trying to slow him down, but he only pulls harder. I kick up my leg and grab the hunting knife secured to my leg. I flip him over my head, dragging the knife across his throat once he's on the ground in front of me. He gurgles and writhes against me as the blood pours from the gaping wound. I pull a gun from its hiding place on my other leg and point it to the guy who's struggling to get to his feet after his massive crash. Shards of glass from the shattered coffee table cover the floor, and Uncle Gio stares at me, his eyes wide.

I smirk at him. "Wanna tell me again how destroyed you are over this? How we're fucking blood, you slimy piece of shit?" I inch closer to him, my voice dropping. The idiot who was supposed to take me out struggles to his feet, and I don't even look at him when he goes for his own gun. I point and shoot twice. Out of the corner of my eye, I see him collapse to the floor, his brain matter now decorating the upholstery.

Just a little bit of redecorating.

The place needed a few updates anyway.

Gio cowers against a stone wall, whimpering like a little bitch.

"Tell me again, old man!" I yell. "How we're family?"

"I didn't do it, Cristian!" he cries, full on sobbing now. "I swear, I didn't do it!"

"But you know who did, motherfucker. And you're gonna give me a name right now!"

"I d-don't have a name!"

"Bullshit!" I press the barrel of the gun against his temple. "Tell me who did it, Gio! Or I'll mount your fucking head on this wall after I cut it off your body!"

He covers his face, shoulders quaking with sobs that get louder with each passing second. "I only did what they told me to do! I only told them where to find him, nothing else!"

"And how much did they pay you?" I hiss, smacking the gun against his temple.

"A million dollars," he weeps. "Oh God, I'm so sorry! I didn't want to do it, but I needed the money and—"

"You could have come to us if you needed money!" I yell into his face. His eyes are red and puffy, and I know he's really sorry.

Well, at least sorry he got caught.

Too little, too late.

"Where did the money come from?" I snarl through gritted teeth. "Give me a name and I'll let you go. Then we'll find the bastard together. You'll help me take whoever it is down." Not that I have any intention of making good on my bullshit offer to him, but I need the goddamn name so I'll tell him just about anything right now. Lucky for me he's too fucking stupid to realize he won't be leaving this little slice of heaven overlooking the Mediterranean.

And actually, lucky for *him* I'm not dipping his ass in chum and anchoring him in the sea so that sharks can feed on him.

Uncle Gio nods, his breaths short and sharp. "O-okay, Cristian. Thank you! I will help you. Of course, nephew. I am so sorry to have betrayed you."

"Shut the hell up and give me the name!" I shout.

He nods, taking a few deep breaths. "Yes. It was—"

Crack!

My uncle's body goes limp and slides to the floor, blood pouring out of the wound on his forehead.

About an inch away from where I'm standing.

I dive to the ground as the stone wall behind me is peppered with bullets. Uncle Gio lands next to me, his eyes open wide. It creeps me the fuck out, but I don't have time to stare. I need to find whoever just put a bullet between my uncle's eyes.

Primarily because I don't need one between my own.

A few more gunshots crack behind me, smashing glass sculptures and picture frames.

Pop! Pop! Pop!

I creep around a chair close to the front door and then run past it, crouching low to the floor. More gunshots pierce the air and bullets tear through the foyer. I dodge them all, my chest tight. I sink to the floor to reload, shoving in another magazine. I cock the gun and point it straight out. A shadow hovers just outside one of the front windows. I can see a dark figure through the slit in the red and gold curtains covering the glass panes.

He's waiting.

I'm waiting.

I need answers.

He doesn't want witnesses.

I eye the front door. He won't come inside. He's waiting for me to come out so he can put me into a shallow grave next to my uncle.

Screw that.

He takes a few steps closer to the door, his back to me.

I have only seconds to attack.

Shock and awe.

They never see me coming.

I draw in a deep breath and leap toward the window, kicking through the glass with my feet. I drop to the ground and roll to my feet, firing three shots at my assailant. One to the shoulder, two to the chest.

More than enough to make him crumble to the ground.

But none of them kill shots.

Not yet.

I want a fucking name!

His gun clatters to the cobblestone path and I kick it away, falling to my knees. I grab a fistful of his greasy hair and yank so he can see my face.

"Who sent you?" I yell, sticking my finger into one of the bullet holes in his chest.

He winces but stays silent.

I press harder and still nothing. It pisses me the fuck off, so I launch a fist at his pock-marked face.

"Fuck you," he grows, spitting at me.

"Who do you work for?"

"Not for you, cocksucker." His breathing is labored, and I slam his head back so it cracks against the cobblestone path. Nothing...until he laughs. A slow, sinister, psychopathic laugh that makes the rage bubble in my veins.

"Who sent you?" I scream into his face.

His hands clamp to the sides of my head and he brings my face down to his, his teeth clamping onto my ear and tearing at the flesh.

I stick my finger back into his bullet wounds and he releases my head. I jump back, kicking away from him. I fire off as many shots as I have left until his 'roided-up body goes slack, blood from my goddamn ear drizzling down his chin. I put a hand to it, clenching my fists. I walk over to him and kick him in the head.

As hard as I can.

I do it again and again and again.

But it doesn't make me feel whole. It doesn't make me less sad or less angry or less betrayed.

It's just a harsh reminder that I fucked up the one lead I had for my father's murder. I didn't come here to find out why my uncle betrayed us. I already knew his reason.

Money. It was always money with Gio.

But I can't save my family unless I know who I'm battling. That's the missing link, what I was prepared to beat out of my uncle — the name of the asshole who set out to destroy us.

As I stare at the bullet-riddled man lying at my feet, I realize I'm still no closer to the truth. I still don't know who killed my father.

And now I'm short a fucking ear.

Chapter Four
TALI

My feet pound the pavement, sneakers thumping harder and faster as the seconds tick by. I stare out at the Mediterranean from the safety of the road. The moonlight glitters atop the water like jewels as I expel a deep breath.

Safety.

Ha.

I work my legs until they burn. I need to feel the pain, the scorching assault on my muscles, because it erases everything else.

At least for a little while.

I don't deserve to be free like this.

I'm held captive by a dark secret, and sometimes I'm just tempted to scream it from the hilltops.

But I don't. I can't.

I refuse to let it overtake everything good in my life.

I don't care about myself anymore.

But I do care about my family.

I need them, need to know they're safe.

So I keep the secret buried down deep where it festers and knots my insides every time the images flash across my mind, which is pretty damn often.

I push harder, straining to reach the top of the hill.

Running is my only escape from the reality that stares me in the face every time I look in the mirror.

Every time I look at *him*.

My eyes sting from the gruesome images wallpapering my mind, and I swallow the sob rising in my chest. My foot catches in a crack in the narrow concrete path. I can barely see in this damn dusky light. I gasp, twisting sideways to avoid face-planting in the gravel along the side of the road. A small red sports car careens around a sharp bend, its bright white headlights catching me off-guard, making me stumble backward. It zooms past, pelting me with a gust of wind and gravel in its wake. "Ahh!" I scream, my arms flailing in the air as I spin left and right to regain my balance.

Lucky.

Yeah, great.

I can live another toxic day.

Running out here at night...alone...is just stupid.

I know firsthand what can happen along these steep curves, what can happen if you're not paying attention, and what can happen if you *are*.

My knees shake, legs wobbly. I swipe at my forehead with one of my wristbands, but it's not sweat pouring down my face.

Tears. I've shed so many over the past months.

I always wonder how there could possibly be any more inside of me, but every once in a while, they flood my eyes.

I wish they could carry all of the guilt and sadness with them, but it still remains. It's always inside of me. I fear it always will be.

I huddle into the side of a rocky hill, pulling my sweatshirt tight around me. My teeth chatter as the cool night breeze whispers through my standard running uniform of Lululemon and Under Armour.

I lean my head on the tops of my knees and stare out at the sunset, my finger tracing an outline on the top of my iPhone screen. Just a handful of numbers. That's all it would take.

I could dial those numbers and reclaim my life.

I grab the phone, clenching it tight in my hand. "Goddammit!" I yell, my voice echoing in the still air.

I can't reclaim a single thing. I can't take any of it back. I can ease my guilt or I could rain hellfire down on my family.

Those are my only two choices. There is no middle ground.

Making the call is a selfish move.

Either way, I suffer.

Either way, I'm screwed.

I launch my arm back, gritting my teeth, the urge to hurl the phone over the side of the cliff so powerful.

Just erase the temptation, right?

A faint rustling of leaves makes me leap to my feet. Of course the road is desolate now that I'm completely alone, in the dark, and did I mention alone?

It has to be an animal. Something nocturnal. A bump-in-the-night type of thing.

I squeeze my eyes shut. Christ, I hate animals, but please let it be an animal! A small one, ideally.

I tiptoe away from the place where the leaves shake the most, my eyes darting all around except up above me. I don't see the large, dark figure suddenly falling out of the sky until it lands next, feet-first, and then tumbles into me.

I let out a bloodcurdling shriek, my body airborne, falling backward to the road when a pair of strong arms tighten around me. They take the full impact when we crash to the gravel with a thud, knocking the air completely out of my lungs.

A loud engine roars from behind me, another tiny, overpriced European sports car tearing around the sharp corner, and I yelp, squirming around underneath the dark figure, trying to push myself away...from it *and* the oncoming car. A large hand grips my wrist, yanking me up and pulling me away from the road just as the car swerves around me. The tires screech as the car corners around the curve and zooms past.

I twist and flick my wrist to release the death grip of whoever just saved my life.

Thank you to my dear and lethal cousin Kat for teaching me that very handy move.

With both hands free, I'm at least prepared for what comes next.

Kind of.

I can try to run, but on these dark roads, I won't get very far. And the only way to stop one of these crazy-ass drivers is to leap in front of their cars and pray they see you before bulldozing you.

A pang assaults my chest.

God knows I'm familiar with that whole scenario.

So yeah, I'm pretty much finished if this person has a weapon or any psychotic, murderous tendencies.

I squint in the faint moonlight. How the sky turned from dusk to full-on black so quickly is beyond me. Being lost in my thoughts isn't safe for me, no matter where I am. I jump into a fighter's stance because it's my best bet for survival. I dance backward on my toes, waiting, wishing I had something on me that was a tad more deadly than a driver's license and a key card to my penthouse apartment.

I am a horrible planner.

And in my line of work, I really should know better.

Who knew I'd be out at this hour? In the dark?

I should have been back at the hotel an hour ago when it was still light.

But something brings me back here too often than I'd like to admit.

I don't know what I expect to find.

Redemption? Forgiveness? Freedom?

Instead, I always leave empty-handed and with a heavy heart.

"Easy, Rocky," a low, male voice pants. The dark figure finally speaks and he's out of breath. "I'm not gonna attack you."

But that voice...I recognize the voice...

I take a step closer, still ready to launch a strike with one of my working limbs should the need arise. "Who's there?"

The figure steps out of the shadows, the thin slivers of moonlight shining upon a chiseled jaw...one I've dreamt about for weeks, that is, until the demons took hold of my thoughts.

"Marcone?" I gasp. "What the fuck are you doing out here?" I peer up at the darkened hilltop. "And why were you up in a tree?"

"I'm part of the Audobon Society of Monaco." He adjusts his clothes, his breathing a little calmer. "I was bird-watching."

I roll my eyes and peer at his light-colored shirt, at the splotches of darkness staining them. "You're a mess. What the hell is all over you?" I creep closer still, reaching out a hand without even thinking. I cautiously graze the damp fabric, recoiling as his taut pecs twitch under my curious fingertips. "Eww, it's wet! What the hell is it?" I take a long look and tilt my head up toward his. It's only when he turns his face slightly to the side that I see his ear.

Or what's left of it, anyway.

"I got attacked by a seagull."

"While you were bird-watching. In a tree. At night." I stick my hands on my hips.

"Well, yeah. It couldn't see me, so it felt threatened. Of course it would attack." He shrugs and pulls off the shirt, balling it up in his hand. But he doesn't drop it. He keeps it clenched in his hand.

I nod. "Okay. That's the ridiculous story you're sticking with?"

"Hey, I never said it had a happy ending."

Jesus. He had to say happy ending, right? "Aren't you going to try to stop the bleeding?" I say, trying like hell to drag my eyes away from his Photoshop-perfect sculpted torso.

I want to touch. I want to lick. I want to bite.

I clamp my lips shut to prevent the tiny moan from escaping

Oh, hell.

I hate this guy! I mean, yeah, he saved my life a second ago, but still.

He's a total dick.

I bite down on my lower lip.

Yes. A massive dick with a shredded body I'd love to melt into.

Onto.

Whatever. Semantics.

I want him.

"No." He starts walking down the hill toward the shoreline, headed for his hotel, no doubt.

I furrow my brow. He's a total jerk with absolutely no sense of chivalry. He's just going to *leave* me out here—

He tosses a smirk over his shoulder. I see it clear as day, his eyes twinkling in the moonlight.

Damn that moonlight.

It does crazy things to a person.

"You coming or what?"

I fold my arms over my chest. "I don't need an escort."

He shrugs and keeps walking, still clutching that shirt.

"Why are you taking the shirt with you?" I call out in some lame attempt to stop him. I mean, could I be any more pathetic? He offered to walk me back, and I flat out told him to piss off.

In a more diplomatic way, yes, but still.

Same message.

"It's my favorite."

"Blood stains don't come out easily. You need to know what you're doing."

He stops walking and slowly turns in my direction. "Do you know what you're doing, *Natalya?*"

I take a deep breath. Hell no, I don't! "I've learned some tricks over the years."

That sexy smirk is back. "Oh, yeah? You wanna show me?"

I expel a shaky breath, clutching my arms around me. "Why would I want to help *you*, Marcone?"

He takes a few steps toward me. Slow. Methodical. Each one closer makes my knees quiver to the point where my legs are about to give out.

Badass mafia queen?

Yeah, right. That's me.

If only they could see me now, quaking in my Nikes like a cube of Jell-O.

"Because you want something, something only I can give you."

My mouth drops open, and I snap it closed just as fast. "You're really a piece of work, do you know that?" I scoff. "The only thing I want is for the ground to swallow up you *and* your gaudy monstrosity of a hotel!"

He chuckles, the sound rippling through me like a soothing hum. A shiver slithers down my spine, making me clutch my sweatshirt in my fists.

"I know what you want, Natalya," he murmurs, stopping when he's right in front of me. I tilt my head backward after raking my lust-filled eyes over his ripped chest one more time.

"Oh, you do?" I whisper.

He nods, his face now serious. "Yeah. I do."

"I don't need anything from you," I rasp, his cologne teasing my nostrils. The fresh clean scent catches in my throat as I try to drink it in. My throat tightens as his breath flutters against my face like feathers.

"But you do." His face relaxes into a wicked smile. "Like the strip of land between our hotels. You want to build a restaurant there, right? Another perk for the undesirables your resort attracts so well?"

I jump back with a loud gasp. "You know about that?"

"You filed a petition to gain control of the property." He snickers. "Of course, I know. And I'm the reason why it hasn't gone through yet, if you hadn't already guessed it."

"Oh!" I slam my hands against his chest, pushing him, and I swear this time it's not because I really want to feel his muscles tense against my skin. No, this time I really want to keep him the hell away from me. "You really are an asshole!"

"Why? Because I didn't just bend over and let you grab it? Is that how you like to work, Natalya? Is it all take, take, take with you? You make things happen because you use connections...sound familiar? Are you gonna try to get some of your brothers to muscle me so I let it go?"

Anger floods my veins, and I clench my fists. "I have actual plans for that land, you jerk! You're just being a dickhead because... because..." I slap my hands against my running tights. "Because it's who you are!"

"I don't think that's fair," he murmurs. "Did you really think you were going to grab it right out from under my nose? Is that what your 'connections' promised you? That you could just fly under the radar and they'd take care of everything?" He smiles. "Yeah. I've got the same connections. And they always honor the highest going rate. But maybe we can make a little arrangement. Maybe have a little friendly competition to see who should get it."

"Did you hear me? I have plans! Competition, my ass!"

He peeks behind me, giving an appraising nod. "You don't want to get me started on your ass if you're not gonna deliver."

"I hate you!" I shriek.

"I like this rage I bring out of you." He lifts an eyebrow. "And I'd like to channel it into something a little less deadly, if you're up for it."

"You're so lucky the only thing I have on me right now is my driver's license!"

"If you were any bit skilled, you'd be able to slit my throat with it."

"Oh my God!" I throw my hands into the air. "I am totally going to torpedo your ass with a watermelon if you don't leave me the hell alone!"

"Oohh. We're into the full-blown threats now, huh." He lets out a dry laugh. "*Full-blown*. Now I'm excited."

I push past him in a huff, hating that his condescending laughter only makes me want him more. I break into a swift jog, fighting every cell in my body.

She's a traitorous bitch that wants nothing more than to climb that sexy, delectable mountain of a man.

But fuck her.

And fuck him harder.

Chapter Five
CRISTIAN

I stagger through a private entrance to my hotel about half an hour later, still clutching the balled-up, bloody shirt in my fist.

The walk should have cleared my head, should have cooled me down, should have made me realize what an idiot I am for mentioning anything about that shared land to Tali.

Of course she wouldn't know that I'd already sniffed out her plans.

I wasn't thinking.

I feel like that happens a lot lately.

Maybe I lost too much blood along with the chunk of my ear.

Or maybe just being around her makes me forget why I'm here and what I need to do.

I walk down the hall, running a hand through my hair and grazing my ear by accident. Shit, that burns. "Dammit," I mutter, stabbing the Up button next to my hidden elevator. I don't even want to think about what it must look like in the light.

No, I'd much rather think about Tali and her perfect legs and ass. Just the image of her in those tight pants is enough to make my dick twitch.

I slam my fist into the wall just as the elevator doors open. I step inside and they close, taking me to the top floor.

My brother Diego is waiting for me, lounging on a long brown leather couch overlooking the sea. He twists around when the elevator doors open, his martini sloshing over the sides of the glass. "Fuck me, what the hell happened? Whose blood is that?"

"Not sure. We didn't have much time for small talk before I popped him." I toss the stained shirt on the counter and grab a beer from the stainless steel refrigerator before collapsing next to him. "It was a setup."

He nods. "Not surprising. Gio is a low-life bastard. He sold out Dad. You had to know you'd be next. He'd cut his own mother's throat for a nickel."

"Well, he's not gonna be cutting anything anymore." I take a long gulp of the ice-cold beer and let out a sigh.

"You took him out?"

"Not me." I lean my head back and close my eyes.

"Well, who the fuck did it?"

"I don't know. I was a little busy trying not to get killed myself. Gio had his guys there, ready to pounce. They were pathetic, though." I shake my head. "After I took care of those assholes, I had him. Gio was gonna give me a name. But someone put a bullet between his eyes before I could do the job."

"And your ear?"

I turn to my brother with a half-grin. "Motherfucker took a bite out of it, so I plugged him."

"And lemme guess, that was before you found out who killed Dad?" Diego rolls his eyes. "C, how the fuck are we gonna find those people if you keep killing the damn messengers?"

"He chewed off my ear. I wasn't really thinking straight."

Diego peers at the dried-up blood streaking the side of my neck. "We need to take care of that. You're gonna need stitches. I don't suppose you have the rest of your earlobe in your pocket, do you?"

I take another long sip of my beer. "It could still be in his mouth, for all I know."

"Okay, I'll get the doctor up here. You'll be good as new for the gala." He pulls out his phone and types something onto the screen.

I groan. "What gala? You know I hate black tie."

Diego smirks at me. "Well, get used to it fast. We're saving the ocean, bro."

"Why do we need to be there? We've got other things to handle."

"Because we need to show the people here that we're legit, C. That this *empty* hotel isn't a complete bullshit cover for our operations. Whoever put the hit on Dad back in Sicily is the same person who killed his partner, Daniel Tava. Right here in Monaco. They took them both out so they could grab full control of the shipping business. We find one, we find both."

"Yeah," I grumble, rubbing the back of my neck. "I guess you're right."

"You *guess*?" Diego lifts an eyebrow.

I let out a deep sigh. "Fine! I *know*!"

"That's better. I know you hate to wear a tux, but we have to be at that gala. And we need to fly under the radar this time." He gives me a pointed look.

"It's not like I expected to have some guy's head explode all over me."

"I think it's safe to say that wherever you are, bloodshed will usually follow."

I wink at him. "That's my MO."

"Get a new one for the gala." Diego paces in front of the windows. "Daniel Tava's death wasn't an accident, C. I don't give a fuck what the papers say. Hit and run, my ass. It was planned. Everyone in the world knew he was here for that dinner with the prince. He was being tracked every step he took until the night he just so happened to be out walking by himself. No way was that an accident. And when we find the person who did it, we'll know exactly who went after Dad. And the gala is a perfect place for us to get information. I guarantee whoever railroaded Tava's ass will be there clinking fucking glasses with whoever else is involved."

"Okay, Columbo. Point taken." I scrub a hand down the front of my face. "You're probably right. Uncle Gio has a hard-on for that shipping business. *Had* a hard-on is more like it now. He knew how much cash it was bringing in and how much more we'd see once we expanded into Asia."

"Exactly. Together, Dad and Daniel ran the coast of the Mediterranean. Their combined shipping business is worth billions, and it won't be long before the scavengers come to feed off of what's left." Diego stands up and goes over to the bar to mix himself another drink. He really is smarter than anyone gives him credit for. Sometimes I think he likes that. Makes him feel like more of a threat. He also likes to shock the shit out of people, too. It's all about strength and power. The less people expect of you, the more scared they are when they see what you're actually capable of doing. "And that's why we need to be at that gala. You've already made some contacts in the government, right? That's exactly what we need to keep doing... making ourselves known. We show them what value we can bring to this place, and they decide they need to keep us here doing our business. More business equals more money for them. More money for them is incentive for them to give us information when we need it."

I gulp down the last of my beer and slam the glass bottle on the table next to me. "People really don't give you enough credit, you know that?"

"My brilliance is my secret weapon," Diego says with a smirk. "They never see me coming. People aren't threatened by me until I want them to be."

"The humility. I mean, wow." I shake my head and snicker. "How the fuck does your head fit through the goddamn door?"

"Just be thankful I'm on your side."

"Sure, I'll just drop to my knees right now."

"Smart ass. See, this is why you're not the strategy guy. All you care about is how many kills you get. You don't think long term. You don't see the bigger picture. And you definitely aren't the one to make friends."

"Fuck friends. We're here to find Dad's killer! A rat bastard murderer who's plotting against our family with the help of who the hell knows how many other groups. And you expect me to sit on my hands and wait for you to 'think things through'? Sorry, Diego. I don't waste time thinking. I act because it's the only way to hold the lead in this game."

"You can't blow our cover; otherwise, we will fail. Do you get that? This isn't about revenge! It's about protecting the rest of our family and our livelihood! For as many associates as Dad had, he had three times the number of enemies, all drooling over the chance to grab a slice of his money pie. That's our target, and if we shake shit up, they'll scatter like goddamn cockroaches."

"It's a big target. You know there are only two of us here, right? I mean, your big brain may count as three people, but we're still at a little bit of a disadvantage."

"Tommy, Vince, Anthony, and Gianna have their parts handled back home. If you play by the rules for once in your fucking life, we will win. So you're gonna wear the tux, shave the goddamn scruff, and smile like you actually mean it. Hell, I don't care if the reason you smile is because of all the heads you plan to chop off in the next few weeks. Just do it. Charm the shit out of whomever you need to. We're close, C. Don't lose it yet."

Ding!

I look up at the security camera. The doctor is on his way up.

I cock an eyebrow at Diego. "Okay, let's see if the Doc can help me clean up before the big event."

Diego nods. "That's better. Play by the rules this time. Otherwise, next time, it might be more than just your ear that gets bitten off."

Speaking of biting, there's only one other place I wouldn't mind a little bit of a nip and tug.

But it sure as hell doesn't involve death.

Just a little foreplay.

With none other than Tali Severinov.

Chapter Six
TALI

My head is spinning...out of control...can't stop it...can't stop... I clutch the sides of my head, pressing my fingertips to my temples, willing the images swimming in front of my eyes to stay still for a second.

But they don't.

They flash across my eyes, swirls of bright lights, blurs of color. I can't focus, my breaths coming fast and furious in short, harsh gasps. I squeeze my eyes shut, but it only makes the spinning worse.

Faster.

Harder.

More violent.

My mouth is dry, filled with imaginary cotton. I can't speak, can't weep, can't formulate a single thought.

I jerk back and forth, my shoulder slamming into something hard and sharp.

My mouth drops open to let the scream escape, but it catches in my throat, a garbled knot of sounds that nobody will ever hear.

Nobody...because it's the end.

I sit straight up in my bed with a loud yelp, yanking the bedsheet up to my neck. A deep chill settles into my bones as it always does when the demons come to visit each night. They never quite catch me...I always wake up before they can reach out and make contact.

But I know deep down it's only a matter of time before they do.

Tears sting my eyes, and I berate myself again for ending up in this place.

The whole *I was sad and he was charming and sweet* doesn't count for a goddamn thing anymore. It hasn't for a while now. I knew what I was getting into. Or, at least, I thought I did. I needed a distraction, a new focus, and Alain was it.

He said all the right things, did all the right things, and basically charmed me out of my panties. Unfortunately, he's done the same thing to about ten other A-list celebrities in the time we've been together.

That I've seen on the Internet, anyway.

God only knows how many more there have been offline.

My brothers hate him, naturally. They don't understand why I won't break away...why I can't break away. They worry about me, but the ironic thing is that I'm only staying with Alain because I'm worried about *them*.

I swing my legs over the side of the bed and stand up, stretching my arms overhead. I didn't hear from Alain last night. That's not like him. He always calls to check in on me.

Not because he really gives a shit about me, but because he gives more of a shit about himself.

I thought he really did care about me once upon a time. He was the doting, supportive, and concerned boyfriend...until he wasn't. Or rather, until he'd gotten what he needed from me. But it wasn't enough. He couldn't risk me walking away, not with everything that was at stake, so he reeled me back in.

Only this time he didn't do it with lavish gifts and vacations and promises of forever.

He used a different tactic...one that can tear everything good in my life away from me.

But because of it, somebody wants me dead.

Maybe more than one somebody.

All because of what I've done. What I've seen. What I can't admit to, no matter how tempting it is to finally be free of this noose around my neck.

Every day, it pulls a little tighter.

One day, it's going to choke the life out of me for good.

There won't be any second chances. No hope for redemption.

I'm too far gone for that.

The evidence tells me they're closing in. They've proven they can get close.

The big question is, what are they waiting for?

I pad into my lavish white bathroom. Every inch of the space is covered in Italian marble, save for the porcelain tub in the center of the floor. I open the tall linen closet and furrow my brow. No towels?

I let out a deep sigh and go into the bathroom down the hall and open the closet, pulling out two fluffy white towels. I pad back into my bathroom and turn on the shower, watching the steam rise from the glass enclosure.

The front door slams, and I jump. Who the fuck—?

I pull open the door slowly, trying to hear over the sound of the rushing water.

Alain's voice rises, echoing in the hallway. "What the hell are you talking about?"

I tiptoe into the hall, concentrating on what's coming out of his jerkoff mouth. "He was given specific instructions!" Pause. "I don't care who was there! Everything was left behind!"

I chew my bottom lip. Who is he on the phone with at this hour? It seems a little early to get this crazy about work. This is my hotel, and it was just bombed, for chrissakes. You don't see me getting all whacked-out over the renovations. Although, I haven't had my coffee yet.

I guess it *could* happen after I'm properly caffeinated.

"Well, make sure they know it. And don't call me again until it's done." He clicks the end call button, and I lounge against a wall, waiting for him to turn around and notice me standing there. He dicks around with his phone for a little while longer, cursing in French. I watch him pace in front of the television in the living room, muttering, his face twisted into a grimace.

He must be pretty deep in thought because he still hasn't looked up.

And I don't know why he's even here.

We have an arrangement, yes.

But there's nothing remotely intimate about it.

Not anymore.

"What the hell are you doing here, Alain?" I ask, folding my arms over my chest.

He turns to me with a look of disdain. "That's probably the last thing you need to be worried about right now, Tali."

"What's that supposed to mean?" I snap, stomping toward him. I know his game, and I'm tired of it. For weeks, I've been looking over my shoulder, wondering where, when, how…I need to end this. Once and for all. I have to escape.

He drags a finger down the side of my arm, digging it in hard. I shake it off. I don't want any of his disgusting tentacles coming near me ever again. "I think you need to be more concerned about the future of your hotel. And everything else you love in this life."

The blood chills in my veins. "What are you saying?"

He creeps closer to me, his eyes narrowed to little black slits. "I'm saying that if you get any bright ideas about going public with what you know, just remember that the little renovation project you're doing downstairs, courtesy of that bomb, will be nothing compared to the leveling I give this place."

My mouth drops open. "What are you saying?" A hoarse whisper. It's all I can muster.

The corners of his lips curl into a sinister smile. "I think you've finally figured it out. Bravo, darling. I was wondering if I'd have to spell it out for you."

I take in a sharp breath. "But it was your car…and you turned my hotel upside down! People could have been hurt…or killed!"

Alain shrugs. "They would have been unfortunate but necessary casualties. Lucky for you, the only real loss was my fucking car, which you need to file a claim for, by the way."

"Screw your goddamn car!" I screech, shoving my hands against his chest and pushing him backward. "This is my *life*, you bastard!"

"Exactly," he sneers. "It is your life. And if you want to keep it, you'll do exactly as I say. And *I* say keep your fucking mouth shut." He holds up a hand in front of my face. "No, no, no. Don't you dare say what you're thinking right now. I can see the wheels turning. There is no way to escape this, Tali. You know exactly what will happen if you try." He puffs out his chest, his eyes meeting mine. We're the exact same height. I should have known when I met him that he'd have a Napoleon complex and I should run far and fast. Too little, too late for me. He has me. He knows it. I know it. And the only people who don't know it are my brothers.

The three reasons why I keep my end of the deal.

Actually, scratch that. It's not a deal. In a deal, I'd be benefiting.

This is fucking blackmail. Plain and simple.

He winds a strand of my hair around his finger and tugs it hard, grinning. I wince, biting my lower lip to keep the expletives from flying out of my mouth. "I remember you liked it when I'd pull your hair while we fucked." He sticks out his tongue and drags it down the side of my face. I squirm out of his grip and crack my fist against his jaw. It wasn't a kill punch. I don't need that shit, especially now.

I'll reserve it for later. When he's expecting it. That's the only fun way to deliver one of those.

I want him to see it coming.

I want him to know that his lights are about to flicker out.

Permanently.

But this punch? It was weak. He doesn't even flinch. He just laughs and rubs the side of his face. I hope it turns into a rainbow of disturbing shades. He's such a narcissist. Any physical imperfections drive his pint-sized ass crazy. "Did that feel good, Tali?" He hisses, so close to my face that my cheek gets splattered by the anger dripping from his lips. "Do you feel like you got back some control right then?" He backs me against a wall, pressing me against it with his chest. I clench my fists. I could split this bastard in half, except I don't know who'll show up in my demolition zone next looking for vengeance. Until I do, I have to play by his rules. Let him think he's calling the shots.

But he'll never be the victor. Over my dead and rotting body will I let him win. I grit my teeth, refusing to answer him.

He taps the side of my face with his index finger. "Guess again, darling. You don't have a fucking shred of it. Not one single crumb. You're going to keep that pretty mouth shut unless you want me to shove my cock into it, do you understand?"

"Fuck you," I seethe before turning my head and seizing his thin finger in my teeth. I bite down hard, so hard I almost immediately taste blood. He screams something in French, tugging it from my teeth's monster grip. He raises a hand, ready to launch a punch at the side of my head to coax my teeth into releasing its victim.

Idiot. Like I didn't see *that* coming a mile away.

This guy is a shady sonofabitch when it comes to business, but I can flatten him like a bug in a hot second.

Again, *how* the hell did I get sucked into his sugary crusted crème brûlée façade?

Fucking frog.

There's no princess on the damn planet who can erase the ugliness of this bastard with a kiss, that's for shit sure.

A loud rapping on the door is the only thing that stops him from taking the shot. With a murderous glare, he shoves past me and grabs a hand towel from the kitchen. He wraps his bloody finger tight, leaving a trail of drops along the polished tile floor.

My heart thumps hard, panicked thoughts blasting through my mind like rogue bullets.

Alain planted that bomb. That sonofabitch! He'd let me believe it was someone else, someone who knew.

Someone who saw.

Someone who was coming to collect.

Without another word, he struts back into the living room where he left his phone. I wipe the blood from my mouth with a paper towel and run to the door, flinging it open.

I want to cry with relief when I see my brother Kaz leaning against the wall, scrolling through his phone. He looks up and smirks at me. "You ready to get your ass kicked?"

I throw my arms around his neck and he pulls me close. "What's wrong, Tal?" he murmurs as I bury my head into his broad shoulder.

"Nothing," I whisper. "Just glad you're here."

"Remember, you've only got me for another day. I'm flying back tomorrow. Meeting Lindy in Ibiza while she's on break from classes."

Lindy is Kaz's girlfriend, a badass Italian princess whom he busted for counting cards at his casino last year. I've never seen a woman bring my brother, the contract killer, to his knees so willingly.

They're a match made in mafia heaven.

"Right," I whisper into his neck. "I forgot."

Footsteps click along the tile behind me, but I don't look up. I know it's that sniveling cocksucker, and I can't bear to look at him again. I need him the hell out of here before I break down and lose my shit here in the doorway. I need to go to the gym with my brother and put Alain's disgusting face on a heavy bag. That way, I can pound the hell out of it, just the way I imagine I'll have the opportunity to do soon enough.

"What's up, LePrick?" Kaz sneers at Alain.

"Stop," I mumble. "Just let him leave."

"What happened to your finger?" Nope. After all these years, Kaz still hasn't learned the meaning of the word 'stop.' "You get a little too crazy with the brie and croissant preparation this morning?"

Why do I bother?

I nudge him and straighten, twisting my head in Alain's direction. God, I want to see him dead.

How much longer do I need to suffer before that becomes a possibility?

Alain steps forward, his nose in the air. It's his best attempt at full height, not that he can even reach the shoulders of my massive brother.

I'm telling you. He's Napoleon.

Reincarnated.

In the flesh.

Speaking of flesh...

Kaz cocks his brow. "I've never seen anyone lose that much blood using a cheese cutting knife. Maybe it's time to learn how to use the big boy utensils."

Of course he picks this exact time to make that kind of an observation.

Jesus Christ...

Alain's lips stretch into a straight line. "So quick witted, Ivan Drago. Looking at you, nobody would ever guess it."

Kaz's face twists into a grimace. "And looking at *you*, Kermit, nobody would ever believe there's a dick tucked into those pants."

Alain lets out a dry chuckle. "And there we go, back to what you do best because you're just not smart enough to do anything more." He looks at me once more, brushing his wet lips against mine, clamping my bottom lip in his teeth before pushing past Kaz. "I'll be back later, after my meeting. We can talk more then."

"Can't wait," I grumble.

Kaz narrows his eyes at me and turns toward Alain's retreating back for one more potshot. "How are you getting to your meeting since your ride's more well-done than Notre Dame?"

The elevator dings, and Alain doesn't respond. He just sticks out his hand, flipping Kaz off before the doors close.

"I can't stand that asshole," Kaz mutters, walking past me into the apartment. "Do you have any juice?"

"Is that your new code word for vodka?" I say with a smirk. "Because the answer, of course, is yes. Or do you just want to mix it with some orange juice because it's only eight o'clock in the morning?"

Kaz walks around the kitchen island, frowning at the floor. "I don't mix. Ever. We're Russian, for fuck's sake. Not pussies." He bends down, pointing to the drops of blood peppering the floor.

"If that soap-dodger was cutting up brie, why is there blood over here?"

"He never actually said he was cutting brie, did he?" I ask, examining my nails.

Kaz jumps to his feet. "So what the hell happened?" His blue eyes darken. "Whose fucking blood is this? Did he hurt you? Oh Christ, tell me he tried something, Tal. Tell me, please, so I can go and pound his snail-snapper ass into oblivion!"

I let out a sigh and pull out a glass. Why did I even open my big mouth like that? Now I have to backpedal and hope he swallows my bullshit excuse. I pour a shot of vodka and hand it to him.

"He didn't do anything. I promise you that."

"And the blood?"

I shrug. "I guess I bit him a little too hard before when we were—"

Kaz's jaw drops. Sometimes it's just better to tell the truth and let the imagination wander. "I think I just threw up a little in my mouth, Tali. I didn't need fucking details!"

"If I was giving you details, I'd just tell you that—"

"Stop!" He takes the glass from my hands and slugs it back. "I'm gonna need about five more of these to get that image out of my head," he groans.

"But we're going to the gym."

"Look at me. Do you think it's gonna have any effect on this?" He smacks his taut midsection.

I smile. "I don't know. Are you ready for *this*?" I smack my own hard midsection.

Kaz shakes his head and picks up the bottle of vodka, pouring his second shot and shooting it. "Almost. Just a couple of more to erase the rest."

"You know, you're definitely a fan of the overshare. Why am I always the one silenced?"

"Because you're my sister." He squeezes his eyes closed. "Now shut up while I drink. You're getting close to the danger zone again."

I roll my eyes. "You're so ridiculous. I'm going to change while you soak your brain in alcohol."

"Good plan. For both of us."

I guess my relaxing shower is going to have to wait.

Too bad since I'm hella tense right now.

Wound like a top.

Alone in my misery.

Dammit, I need a plan!

Living each day, overshadowed by guilt and fear...Jesus, it's like dying a slow and torturous death.

Much like the one I want to inflict on Alain.

Once I find out whom he's working with and why he targeted *me*.

God, I've made so many mistakes in the past year. My spine tenses as I pull on a pair of Lululemon leggings and a sports bra. I'd just wanted to fulfill Dad's legacy. He wanted this resort to be the ultimate luxury destination in Monaco. A five-star, celebrity-chef run restaurant was the last finishing touch on his vision. My stomach clenches. A vision he'd never get to witness. And Michel Dubois, the asshole from the surveyor's office who was supposed to help me claim that piece of land for the restaurant, was my first step in making inroads into the corrupted government.

Because I needed information, and he held the key to the kingdom.

Dad had plenty of his own connections in the government, but they don't owe me a damn thing. I need to start from scratch, creating my own relationships, making my own allies so I can thrive here.

I messed up, though. I made a horrible choice that poisoned my livelihood and the livelihoods of everyone I love. I squeeze my eyes shut as the memories wash over me like a tsunami.

And my sins are going to cost me not only the land, but the answers I know the government holds about that night.

The night that haunts my dreams.

The night when Alain grabbed control of my life.

And that's why I'm going to the gala to save the ocean.

That kind of event is a playground for the biggest political scumbags on the planet. They meet, they wine, they dine, they make deals.

And I have a deal of my own to make.

I just need to find a willing partner.

Chapter Seven

CRISTIAN

Bright colored lights flash across the sky at the open air Opera Garnier, the exclusive location for the Save the Ocean gala. I can see them from a mile away. Vittorio, our driver, takes the sharp turns like the pro he is, whipping the car around curves toward our very elite destination.

"So I guess there won't be any plastic straws tonight, huh?" I say to Diego, whose nose is buried in his phone. I nudge him, but he doesn't respond. "Stop fucking around on Tinder and talk to me."

Diego looks up with a smirk. "I didn't realize you were so needy. Maybe you're the one who should be on Tinder."

I roll my eyes and push back my hair. As if I need any more headaches. I don't have to schedule pussy. If I want it, there is plenty available for me to pound—anywhere, anytime, any way. "Just tell me the plan, okay? No more secrecy. If you're sending me into this thing, at least give me the end game. I don't want to be in there all night, stroking asses. I wanna get in and get out."

He slides a button to raise the partition, leaving Vittorio by himself up front. "I've already gotten a look at the guest list. All of your pals in the government will be there, so the first objective is keeping shit with Gio buried."

I snicker. "No pun intended."

Diego nods, a serious look on his face. "Tell anyone who asks that we were estranged for years because of a falling out he had with Dad. Period. Didn't know he'd be here. Since there are so many tourists in for these events, the media isn't playing up the story. Nobody likes to hear that there's a murderer on the loose when they're working the party circuit all day and all night. Besides, there aren't any witnesses, so you're clear there."

Fuuuuuck.

Technically, he's right. But there was one very curious pair of eyes on me that night.

They're seared into my memory.

And I've been thinking about them ever since.

Not that I bothered mentioning anything to Diego.

Tali seemed to be occupied with her own baggage that night, so I figured I could just fly under the radar with the bird-watching excuse.

She didn't buy it because it was asinine, but she didn't press me on it either.

We both have skeletons and secrets. That much is obvious.

People in business here seldom have empty closets.

And Russian women don't typically wear badges of honor inked into their skin unless they do work that justifies them.

It may have been dark that night, but I'm not blind. And Tali wasn't exactly careful about keeping her sweatshirt zipped.

We both noticed things and chose to ignore them. It was just simpler that way.

I rub the back of my neck.

I think her attention was diverted well enough when I pretty much told her I was stealing rights to the land she's after by using her contacts in the government against her.

I'm sure that didn't piss her off at all.

"Why do you look like you just realized you fucked a tranny in the ass?"

An exasperated sigh passes through my lips. "There may have been a witness. Kind of."

Diego narrows his eyes and leans forward, grabbing the sides of my tuxedo jacket. "What do you mean, kind of?" he asks through clenched teeth.

"It's possible that on my way down from the chalet I may have run into someone."

Understatement of the year.

"Run into whom, exactly?"

"Natalya Severinov." She'd appreciate the use of her formal name since she's made it blatantly clear we are not or never will be *friends*.

Diego's expression goes blank for a split second and then turns murderous. "Tali? Are you fucking kidding me?"

"Not kidding." I shrug out of his grip. "Stop fucking manhandling me, Diego. I made up some bullshit excuse about why I was there."

"With a chewed-up ear."

I snicker. "Well, that explained all the blood on my clothes."

"Jesus Christ!" Diego throws up his hands and then covers his face. "Do I really have to clean up all of your messes, C? Is there gonna be a point in our lives when you actually do what you're supposed to do and not have enough loose ends left to knit a goddamned blanket with?"

"That was a pretty good analogy." I snort. "Are you a ninety-year-old grandma? Knitting? Seriously?"

"You're a real jackass. You got her involved. That means her brothers are gonna know about what happened, too. They're smart people, Cristian. Not the dumb-fuck type we're used to dealing with. And for all we know, they could be involved. That's not good for us. Word gets around. Networks are tight, and we're still building one here. They're already established. Especially her brother Alek."

"How the hell do you know so much about them, anyway?"

"Because I study people! This is our business! I talk to people, I read shit. I learn because it's the only way to keep a leg up!" He shakes his head and groans. "All muscle, no fucking common sense," he mutters.

"It's so damn ironic that everyone thinks you're the idiot."

"I like to keep people on their toes. It gives me an edge."

The car pulls up to the red carpet leading into the venue. Blacked-out SUVs and limousines line the roads, paparazzi cameras flashing incessantly. There are television cameras along both sides of the walkway and photo booths set up where celebrity attendees are being photographed.

It's a madhouse, and it's exactly the last place I want to be right now.

I want to find the fuckers whom my uncle was working with. He put a hit on me...but who was gonna carry it out?

Diego wants names, and so do I. But damn, that rage bubbles beneath the surface, and I can't promise if I came face to face with my own personal assassin that I wouldn't put a bullet between his eyes first and ask questions *never*.

I push open the door and slide out of the backseat, fixing my jacket now that I'm out of Diego's grip. He hops out of the car after me and we move quickly down the red carpet. People in our line of work don't like being out in the open. It's much safer to be in a crowd.

You never know when you might be targeted by a sniper.

We slip past the photogs and their blinding flashes and enter the main area of the gala. The place has been transformed into some kind of undersea fantasia. Blacklights illuminating ocean life as it swims past. Glowing papier Mache jellyfish dance overhead, swaying around in the cool breeze. Crystal chandeliers glitter, alive with color, and candles float in the center of large, glass enclosures, casting a soft glow over the space.

Ostentatious as hell.

Why didn't the foundation just use the fucking money that they spent on all of this bullshit to help the ocean? Did we really need to pay five hundo a plate to come here and pontificate about why we need to save ocean life when we could have just given the ocean everything in the first place?

I don't have patience for this shit.

It's why I'm a liability to my family.

You need someone dead?

Done. I'm your guy.

But if you want me to mix and mingle and commiserate with all of the richest people in the world about how badly the ocean needs us, when they could probably bankroll the whole project their damn selves without even blinking?

Yeah, I'm definitely *not* your guy for that shit.

But here I am. Not because I give a flying fuck about the ocean. Hell, I don't even like to swim in it since I almost drowned as a kid.

No, I'm here for my dad. For my brothers. For my sister.

I'm here for my family.

I'm here for answers.

I'm here for the truth.

"I'm going to make the rounds," Diego nods toward a group of swizzle-stick models across the room. "They look like they need a drink or two."

"I get it. Brilliant cover. Hook in the women, spin them around the floor a few times. Get the attention of your targets." I nod. "They welcome you because of the arm candy you're swinging around. You're in."

"Bingo." He winks at me. "And afterward, I'll show them how grateful I am to the ladies for their assistance."

My brother has this shit down to a sick and deviant science.

It's damn impressive.

I watch him approach the women and they fall over themselves trying to get close to him. With his height, mass, and dimples, women usually react in that way. He's the charmer in the family.

Not me.

I walk over to the bar, scanning the room as I cross the dance floor. It's dark enough that I don't really recognize anyone, so I guess that's a good thing for me. Makes me more anonymous.

Maybe I can get away with not having to make a whole lot of bullshit small talk tonight.

Maybe I can—

I turn around to grab the attention of a bartender when a sharp pain shoots across my foot. "Ahh!" I yelp. Something is stabbing the center of my foot. Hard. Like a knife. I try to pull my foot away from whatever is impaling it, but it's stuck. Like really fucking stuck. I swing around to my right, crashing into the person next to me.

"Could you please move your goddamned sh—?"

The owner of the shoe spins around, a murderous expression on her face. "Do you mind? I was waiting!"

Tali.

Natalya.

Standing on my foot.

Actually, piercing the skin of my foot is much more appropriate. Are there spikes on her shoes?

"Your shoe," I rasp, clutching the bar and trying not to scream in agony.

"What about it?" she snaps.

"It's slicing through my skin."

She looks down, her jaw dropping. "Oh, no. I'm so sorry." Then she looks back at me, eyes narrowed. "Wait. No. I take that back. Not sorry at all."

"I don't care if you're sorry or not. Just move your foot."

"Say please," she sing-songs.

"Please," I grunt, only because I have to. I'm not kidding. I think she may have lanced through the top of my shoe. I could swear she drew blood with those things. She'd be invincible with those shoes as weapons alone.

Suddenly, the intense pain dissipates. The heel lifts, and I can breathe again.

"How's your ear?"

"It still works."

Tali narrows her eyes at me. "What are you doing here? Looking for more people to stuff into your back pocket?"

I furrow my brow, giving her a mock quizzical look. "No, I'm here for the gift bags. I've heard they're giving out Gucci paper straws, AirPods, and Swarovski crystal fish necklaces this year."

She doesn't look amused. "You're screwing with my business."

I'm about ninety-nine-percent certain she's contemplating a way to pull off one of her shoes and stick it in my eye without anyone noticing.

"Isn't this what they call competition?"

"No," she seethes. "It's called cheating."

"You cheated first. But let's face it, I called you out for going behind my back and you didn't like it." I lean closer, catching a whiff of her perfume. God, she smells so fucking good. I want to bury my face in her neck and devour her even though I'm pretty sure she'd harpoon me if she had the chance.

And the weapon in hand.

Her eyes pop open wide, and I smile. She's got that spark for sure. And I feel like it's close to igniting. I want to see those flames roar, so I keep going, at great risk to my other foot. "You thought you'd just flash those eyes and get whatever you want from the people in charge. But they don't care about how you look. They only care about what they can make off of you. You really should know better, Natalya. The one with the biggest stick always wins the game."

Her shoulders square and she narrows her ice blue eyes at me. "The biggest *dick* always wins the game? Is that what I heard?"

I shrug. "If you need more convincing, I'd be happy to show you. But fair warning, you may need a couple of drinks first." My lips curl up into a sly grin. "It's a lot to take in. No pun intended. But it'll be everything you imagined and more."

Chapter Eight
CRISTIAN

I bite back a smile when Tali's nostrils flare. I love that I can have this effect on her. She seems so stiff and stoic most of the time, at least around me. But when I crack through all that, the raw emotion unleashes like a massive storm...directed right at me. She's definitely got a lot of unresolved shit swirling around inside of her. That much is obvious.

Jesus, I want to get this woman on her back so badly so I can fuck the anger right out of her. Minutes, hours, days...as long as it takes.

"What can I get for you?" The tall bartender has finally made his way over to our spot at the crowded bar and is now ready to serve us.

"Vodka on the rocks, please." Tali looks at me like I'm a bug that's just crawled onto her five-hundred-dollar dinner plate. "And he'll take a cold shower. A very lonely one."

"I'm never lonely in the shower," I say with a wink. "But I am thirsty. Macallan, please."

The bartender looks from Tali to me and back, shakes his head, and walks away to get our drinks.

"So how are your renovations coming along?" I ask.

She takes in a sharp breath. "Fine, thank you."

"Do the police have any leads?"

"No." I try to read her expression, but she averts her eyes. There's something festering that she doesn't want me to see, but I'm not in the business of guessing.

I'm in the business of knowing.

"No security feeds, no witnesses?" I lift an eyebrow. "Seems a little odd, don't you think?"

She looks up at me, her glossy red lips stretched into a straight line. "I guess I just didn't pay people well enough for them to divulge information. Maybe I should have taken a play from your criminal handbook instead."

"It's not really a handbook." I smirk. "Just a collection of life lessons, really."

"Oh, really?" Sarcasm drips from her words. "Well, why don't you take your life lessons and peddle them somewhere else instead of polluting my livelihood with them?"

"You'd miss me," I say, my voice husky. "I think you like these little banter sessions. I keep you on your toes."

"Yeah, I'd miss you...like I'd miss having someone cut open my chest without anesthesia." She rolls her eyes and turns away from me when the bartender shows up with two glasses.

He hands them to us and I watch her raise the glass to her painted lips for a sip. She swallows a long gulp, which tells me she needs it. But why? To pretend that she doesn't feel the sizzling charge flowing between us? To keep up her façade of the woman who desperately wants to be taken seriously but doubts every move she makes?

I want to find out more.

But there's one question on the tip of my tongue that begs for an answer before all others.

"Why didn't your boyfriend get that drink for you?" I lift an eyebrow as she chokes a little bit on the next gulp.

She glares at me once it finally makes its way down. "First of all, it's none of your damn business. Let's just get that straight. Second, I am perfectly capable of getting my own drinks."

"Is there more?"

Pink spots color her cheeks. "Third, he's not here."

"He was okay with you coming here, dressed like that, without him?" I take a sip of my scotch and shake my head. "He must be pretty secure."

"How so?"

"Well, either he has a massive cock that he knows will keep you coming back for more or he's got something on you." I snicker. "And since French dudes are usually hung like hamsters, I'm thinking it's the latter."

Her face, which was flushed a few seconds ago, is now bordering on ghostly pale. The color drains from her cheeks and there's no sarcastic comment that follows.

No bitchy retort.

Just stunned silence.

I obviously hit the nail on the head with my observation.

If you pay close attention, you can see a hell of a lot.

My handbook of life lessons.

Maybe she really should read it.

"He had a meeting." She finally speaks, her eyes flickering left and right. "And I don't need his permission about what to wear, where to go, and...and...and anything else, for that matter."

I nod slowly. Very defensive. Interesting. He's got his hooks in her, that's for sure. But does she want them in her? That's the question.

Because I've got hooks of my own. And I know exactly where I want them.

"I'll bet you give him a run for his money."

"What's that supposed to mean?"

"I can tell that you're a woman who knows what she wants. You may stumble getting there, but you won't stop until you do." My eyes are laser-focused on hers, trying in vain to peel away the many layers that lay beyond her hard gaze. But she's not giving up a damn thing.

"You don't know anything about me," she hisses, slamming her glass on the bar.

"Fuck me if I'm wrong, but you're here to make sure I don't get that land. Aren't you? You came alone, in *that* dress, to make yourself known. Because you don't take shit from anyone. And you love a challenge."

"Are you finished with your ten-cent psychoanalysis? I thought you were a hotel proprietor, not a shrink."

"I have a lot of different interests. I dabble in a bunch of areas. Makes me sound worldly."

"So this handbook of yours must have the makings of a bestseller." She tries to fight it, but I've crept under her skin. A smile plays at her lips. I know she hates herself for showing any signs of interest, but it makes my dick twitch.

I'm breaking her down.

She loves the challenge, yes.

But I live for it.

And I won't stop until she begs me to.

"You should read it. I think you'll find it pretty illuminating."

"And how does one get their hands on such a valuable guide?"

"I can give you a map. There are lots of places for your hands to play before they get to seize their prize."

"And are there a lot of hands that have played in these areas before?" Her eyes glitter with mischief.

"Let's just say none have done the job the way I really want. The way I know you would."

With the flick of her hand, she flips her long, caramel-colored hair over one shoulder, staring at my from under thick dark lashes. "It would depend on the value of the prize. If it was really worth my time. Or my *touch*."

My cock springs to life, the reason why I'm here at this event completely pushed to the back of my mind. Tali is now front, center, and spread-eagle on my bed. I don't care about her boyfriend. I don't care about my plans. I don't care about anything right now other than sliding my hands around her back, unzipping that dress, and stripping her out of it. My fingers ache to graze her shimmery skin, to trace the outline of her lips, to knead her luscious tits.

She smiles, taking a step backward. "And I'm not convinced."

With a final seductive smirk, she twists around on her heel and saunters off to a group of men in the corner of the room. I grip my glass tight, adrenaline rushing through me. I fight the urge to grab her and show her how very wrong she is...how worth her time I actually am.

But I stand down.

I don't need to beg.

She'll be back.

And it won't be me doing the begging.

A hand claps me on the shoulder, pulling me out of my X-rated fantasy starring Tali Severinov. A deep voice hums against my ear. "Let's take a walk."

I nod, walking in the direction of the balcony overlooking one of the marinas next to Jak Scala, my trusted confidante and informant. He's the guy who gets shit done. He turns up when I need him and disappears when it's no longer convenient for him to be around.

He gets in and gets out, always managing to stay out of the line of fire.

I, on the other hand, always manage to land right in the center of it.

"Why were you talking to Natalya Severinov?" Jak never beats around the bush. There's no time for that bullshit, not when time is short and we're hunting for the people responsible for my father's death. And since he doesn't pay much attention to my romantic entanglements unless they can help further our business objectives, he must have something.

And judging from the grave look on his face, I don't think my cock is gonna be happy about it.

"She was just apologizing for lancing my foot with one of her heels at the bar."

"Looked like a pretty deep conversation. Were you trying to lance her back?"

"Maybe."

"And yet she walked away. You might want to work a little harder next time you get the chance."

"You think I should take a shot?" I raise my glass to my lips.

"I think it would be worth it."

"Why?"

"Because she's not only a hot piece of ass, but she also has ties to someone you should get a little closer to."

"She's not exactly my biggest fan."

"Has she seen your cock?"

"I've offered, but she hasn't taken me up on it yet."

Jak nods, his lips never giving away any sign of amusement. "Try harder."

"Harder," I snicker, taking another sip. "That's funny."

"Glad you appreciate the joke. Now here's something that isn't funny at all." He leans closer. "The people who ordered the hit on your pop are here in Monaco because you're next on their list, Cristian. You got away from Gio's place, but they're not running away from you. They'll be back. You've done a lot of shit over the years that have pissed people off and they want you out of the picture. You and Diego represent the resistance."

"What about the rest of my family? Tommy, Vince, Anthony, and Gianna? Who's keeping an eye on them back home in Sicily?"

"Don't worry. They've got plenty of eyes on them at all times. But they aren't the ones being hunted. They're running the day-to-day operations there. You and Diego are the ones who are fighting back, who keep asking questions about Daniel Tava, and that's why they're coming for you next."

"Christ only knows who Gio was working with," I grumble. "Cocksucker. I had to keep myself from tearing off his fucking limbs one at a time when he said the word *family* to me."

"Gio was a piece of shit. He was always the guy to follow the money and not care who got fucked in the process."

"Well, this time when he chased the cash, he hit a dead end." I let out a snort. "Literally."

Jak looks at me, his expression impassive. It always is. If the guy has emotions, he sure as hell never shows them. But in his line of work, he needs to keep a clear head. Always. Emotions make you do shit that you shouldn't.

Like kill the assassin who bites your ear off before you can get him talking.

"These people are taking out everyone who was involved with that shipping business. First, your dad. Then, the 'accident' that killed Danial Tava. They want those shipping routes and they will pick off everyone and anyone who stands in their way."

"So who are we dealing with, Jak? Any ideas? Because I sure as hell have none. I've tried to get information from those assholes running the government, but they either don't know shit or I haven't paid them enough to find out details about Tava's hit and run."

"It could be the Russians, the French, the Albanians." Jak shrugs. "They all want those waterways and the ports that come along with them. And when you visited Gio, you terminated everyone who could have given us a name."

I rob the back of my neck. "Yeah, I know. Diego already read me the riot act."

"What happened to your ear, by the way? Did one of your women get a little too hot and bothered?"

I roll my eyes. "One of those nutsacks who attacked me at Gio's chalet bit it, so I shot him in the face."

"You should have had a conversation with him first to figure out who he's working for. Just saying."

"Yeah, well, when you have some douchebag's teeth clamped on your ear, you try thinking straight."

Jak nods. "Noted."

"So what's next? Do I just sit around and play with my dick waiting for the next assassination attempt?"

"No, that's why I suggested you get a little closer to the Severinovs. Alek is big fish in that family. You know him?"

"A little bit. He's kind of a prick, but not a total blowhole."

"Feel him out. Her, too, but not the way your dick wants. Get close, see what they know. They're trying to pick up the pieces now that their dad's gone. New business opportunities, new partners. They've got their hooks into everything right now. And they're big into drug trafficking. They'd profit big time from those ports."

"You really think they might be involved?"

"They may be, they may not be. All I know is that the Severinovs are trying to rebuild their own empire, and drugs play a big part of their business. They also move a hell of a lot of contraband between countries. They'd stand to make a shit ton of cash by taking over those ports. I don't think we can rule anyone out at this point. It's not safe to trust a single person. I'll keep digging. If I can figure out who killed Daniel Tava, then we've got your man." Jak shrugs. "Or woman, as the case could be."

"The case seems pretty air tight to me," I say. "There was no evidence at the scene. No witnesses from what I got from the chief of police. Not a thing."

"There's always something left behind," Jak murmurs, looking around at the still-empty balcony. "We just have to find it. That's my job. In the meantime, you need to keep your enemies close. So close that you can taste them."

"Gladly."

"Don't sample the goods, Cristian. If you let your dick get in the way, we risk a hell of a lot. Your objective is to get Natalya talking. Period. I know Alek, and he's not an easy one to crack. She's your ticket to the inside. Find out who their associates are. Figure out what they know. Be creative. Remember what I said about your enemies."

"Great. And how the hell am I supposed to know who those enemies are?"

"Assume everyone is. That's how you'll survive."

Chapter Nine
TALI

I spot Michel Dubois across the crowded room. He's the center of attention, as usual, holding court with his cronies, talking and laughing loudly.

The guy who can get anything.

Except what *I* need.

I clench my fists. What a pompous asshole. He made a million promises about what he could do for me and my real estate interests, and then delivered on exactly zero of them.

He told me he'd fast-track my survey variance to expand the resort.

He told me not to worry about Cristian's claims to the land, that he'd handle everything, and bury his inquiries with paperwork.

He assured me that my money could get me into...and out of...anything.

And then he took it.

Motherfucker.

I fell for his bullshit. I fooled myself into thinking that I could build up my business and get the protection my family needs when the shit storm blows in.

Knowing Alain, it won't be long. I'm useful to him as long as I keep my mouth shut about what happened that night.

But I'm not stupid. He's going to out me as soon as it's convenient for him.

I have no alibi, and he's got the evidence he needs to sell his story.

It doesn't matter what really happened. Nobody will care. They'll come after me anyway.

I thought if I could get Michel on my side, show him I'm a worthy power player with money to spend, he'd be able to help me somehow—pull some strings, clear my name before it reaches my enemies...

But his promises were all bullshit.

He can't help me.

Or rather, he *won't*, which makes me wonder if my next move will turn out to be a completely lost cause.

Dammit, I hate that I need to start from scratch here in Monaco. My dad's influence didn't exactly transcend his death, and I don't want to have Alek fight my battles for me. I need these dickwads to take me seriously, not look at me like the pretty face who runs back to her family every time things don't go her way.

When I was in Las Vegas, I had my contacts eating out of my hands. They knew what they'd get if they delivered on my requests, and they always came through for me.

But that was different.

I was different.

Ever since I showed up here, constant reminders of my dad assault me like the sharpest of knives, carving away what remains of my already-shattered heart. I carried so much guilt with me after Mom died. Still do. And then not being able to help Dad when he needed it most...

I grit my teeth, an image of Alain's sneering face popping into my mind.

We lost Mom because of me.

I can't be the reason why I lose my brothers, too.

And I need to figure out how to get out of that asshole's clutches without causing any more pain for my family.

I'd hoped Michel would hold the key.

And he does. He's just not giving it up.

I sip my vodka, my eyes scouting the rest of the expansive space at the gala. They land on Cristian.

Of course, there are gorgeous women hanging all over him and the other man standing next to him. My spine stiffens as he places a hand on the back of one of the whores.

I swallow hard, the clear liquid sliding down my throat like water. Christ, when did I become so territorial? It's not fair to call them whores. They might be perfectly nice ladies who aren't angling to ride his alleged massive cock.

The woman leans into him, rubbing her tits against his arm. I can see her hand travel over his thigh until it disappears between his legs.

I roll my eyes.

Right out in the open.

Not whores, my freaking ass.

I bite down on my lower lip to keep the scream from escaping my lips. He's trying to railroad me and crush my business, so what in the hell was he doing cozying up to me at the bar? He already got what he wanted...well, what he *says* he wanted.

And now he's pretty much proven that *he* has Michel Dubois.

Not me.

So what else does he want? To screw me so he can brag that he did it literally *and* figuratively? So that not one single person here takes me seriously ever again?

I know I'm projecting. My livelihood is hanging by a thread, and he's my primary target because I know the risks of letting myself get too close to someone like Cristian Marcone. I know what happens when emotions run wild, and I've already made too many errors in judgment over the past few months because I've been held captive to my own feelings.

He's dangerous.

In more ways than one.

Not that any of it stops the X-rated fantasies from looping through my mind.

God, I hate myself for wanting him so badly. I hate that I'm plotting the death of the bitch who's damn close to dropping to her knees in front of him right now. I hate that he's such a cocky bastard who is trying to kill off the last thing I have left of my dad's...his legacy. But most of all, I hate that I put myself in this no-win situation with Alain where I've become a shell of my former self.

I let him do that to me because I was sad, grieving, and lonely.

Vulnerable.

Weak.

He used it...used *me*...as an opportunity.

I gave him the rope to hang me with and allowed him to take control of my life because of it.

I hate myself for letting it happen!

I hate that he caused so much suffering, that there isn't a damn thing I can do to correct the wrong that's been committed.

A sharp pain in my chest makes me wince.

I can't bring him back.

And the truth can't set me free.

It'll only bury me with him.

My head spins with the countless scenarios where I lose everything, and there are none where I come out on top.

Fuck this! I can't just stand here and wait for things to happen.

I need to make them happen.

I need to grab back some semblance of control.

I need a win!

I slam my glass down on a nearby table and strut toward Michel and his crowd of adoring followers. I swing my hips with each step, making sure that he sees me coming for him. I purposely walk in the direction of Cristian and his admirers, flipping my long hair as I saunter past.

I want him to see me, too.

Michel's beady black eyes rake over my body as I approach and my lips curl into a seductive grin. He moves to the edge of the circle, the drool practically pooling at the corners of his mouth.

Sorry, Cristian. Your cock may be huge, but I have a pussy.

I reach out and put my hand on Michel's arm, my long fingernails grazing the expensive fabric. "Michel," I purr. "So nice to see you." I gaze at him through my thick lashes, and I can suddenly see my path very clearly.

"Natalya," he murmurs, kissing me once on each cheek. The kisses are slow and deliberate, and he takes his time brushing his lips against my skin.

My stomach rolls, but the smile never falters.

"I was hoping we could talk. *Alone*." I tilt my head upward. He's only got an inch on me, but it's enough.

He nods, making me feel like I can say just about anything right now and get him to do it.

Which is exactly my end game.

My eyes betray me for a single second and flick over toward Cristian. His heated gaze locks onto mine, and I can't help but lift an eyebrow in triumph.

He nods with a knowing smile, his slutty sidekick still groping him. Hell, she may even have her hand down his pants.

But he doesn't move his eyes away. He studies me, his gaze searing my insides from where he's standing several feet away. Heat swirls in my belly, and I fight the urge to fling myself into his arms and drop kick his conquest for the night.

I reluctantly pull my gaze back, focusing on Michel.

The object of my desire for control.

I snake my arm through his, leading him away from the group. He doesn't so much as toss back a look to his crew.

Point one, Tali.

I move him toward one of the exits behind the dance floor, my hand pressed to his arm. The cool breeze flutters through my very daring gown. There are cutouts along the sides that run the entire length of my body, leaving very little to the imagination.

And it has the exact effect I'd hoped for.

Michel backs me against the railing once we're outside and away from a sea of curious and intruding stares. "You can't show up here wearing that dress and expect me to keep my hands to myself."

I tilt my head to the side and smile. "Tsk tsk. No self-control at all."

"Not where you're concerned." His hands move up the sides of my torso, his fingers digging into my flesh. The lust in his gaze is all-consuming, but we've already gone down this path and it didn't end well for me.

I need to change the game.

And the rules.

I cover his hands with mine and rest them on my hips, puffing out my chest. His eyes drop to the deep vee of my gown and he licks his lips.

"When do I get a taste, Natalya? How much longer are you going to tease me like this?"

"Oh, Michel," I murmur. "My money wasn't enough for you? You want to up your price now?"

"I want you," he grows, his cock thickening against my leg. "I told you I'd take care of everything, didn't I? Don't flash your pussy at me if you're not going to let me inside."

"What you told me and what you did are two very different things," I say, tracing a finger down the front of his chest. "How am I supposed to trust you now?"

"What are you talking about?" Michel snaps, recoiling slightly. His face flushes red, his mouth twisting into a grimace.

"You're on the take, Michel. And while you collect from everyone, you only deliver to the highest bidder. That's not good business practice, is it?"

His expression darkens in the moonlight, realization settling into his features. "You're no stranger to the way things work around here, Natalya. Everyone has a price."

"Yes, but I paid *your* price," I seethe, poking him in the chest. "With the expectation that you were going to deliver for me. But instead, you chose to deliver to someone *else*."

"I haven't done anything yet. For anyone." He drags a hand down the front of my dress, his fingers tugging at the neckline. "But if you want to up the ante, I'll consider you my top bidder." His hand drops lower, dipping between my thighs. He leans closer, his lips close enough to graze mine.

Bile rises in my throat.

If he tries to kiss me, I will bludgeon him with my shoe.

That is not why I pulled this little stunt.

I wanted to be sure who and what I'm dealing with.

And now I am.

Michel honestly thinks he has the upper hand here.

And he's not afraid of me. At all.

He clearly doesn't see Alek as a threat.

He's a goddamn idiot.

One I can't trust, no matter what price I pay and what currency I use.

"How can I be sure that it will be enough for you this time? That you won't renege on our arrangement?"

He narrows his eyes, rubbing his cock against my leg. "Let's get something straight. You don't make the deals. You take the deals I make. And I only make them if it's worth it for me." His breathing is slightly labored, his eyes a mess of rage and desire. "So you're going to spread those legs for me and show me that you're willing to renegotiate, or you can just leave with nothing. It's your choice. And don't think you can change my mind by threatening to run home to your brothers. I'm not afraid of them. And I have more than enough of my own 'friends' to handle them. And *you*," he sneers. "What's it going to be, Natalya? Are you going to prove to me that you're serious about your hotel's expansion? Or are you just a cock tease who's going to get her tight little ass squeezed out of the circle?"

Holy shit.

A huge blur of red flashes before my eyes, and I flip Michel around so it's his back pressed against the railing. My hand closes around his throat, my nails digging deep into his skin. "Take your fucking hands off me, you sonofabitch. You may think you run this place, but you don't know who the hell you're dealing with."

"Do you think I give a fuck about your goons?" He grabs my hand and pries it off his neck. "Your father knew better than to threaten me. He was a smart man. Are you that smart, Natalya? Because if you are, you'll give me exactly what I want. I can break you. Never forget that."

I grab onto his hand, flip his palm backward and press as hard as I can, effectively breaking his wrist. With a swift motion, I drive my knee into his groin.

Nope, definitely not a pleasant feeling, especially if you've got a stiffy.

Point two, Tali.

He lets out a roar and falls to his knees, clutching his arm to his chest. "You fucking bitch! You're going to pay for that!"

"Oh, yeah?" I ask with a nasty smirk. "Is that price negotiable, too?"

I turn on my heel and storm back into the gala, leaving Michel nursing his wounds. It was a stupid, though necessary, move. He pretty much confirmed that my family influence means shit to him and it won't help me get what I need. I wouldn't have touched his cock with a ten-foot pole, but that wasn't ever my plan. He would just take, take, take, and string me along if I'd let him. So instead, I showed him that I'll get shit done my own way. I may have gotten myself blacklisted by snapping his wrist in two, but at least I learned a couple of lessons in the process.

You can't trust anybody.

And if you need something done, do it your goddamned self.

That's exactly my plan.

My new plan, that is.

Chapter Ten
CRISTIAN

Vittorio hops out of the driver's seat and pulls open my door once we're back in front of my hotel. The gala was still in full swing when I walked out twenty minutes ago, but I'd had enough. Diego couldn't understand why I would ever leave alone when there were so many *desserts* to sample.

But after peeling a pair of hands off of my dick one time too many, I decided pussy wasn't what I needed tonight.

At least, not the pussy that I was being offered.

Unlike Diego, I have standards.

And, so it seems, a death wish.

I was warned by Jak not to dip my wick in the forbidden pool.

I know what can happen if I let myself get sucked in any deeper...who will get hurt.

Or worse.

And for the first time in my life, I don't give a fuck about the consequences.

But *she* doesn't give a fuck about *me*.

That much is obvious.

And it makes the forbidden completely off-limits, which will help me get close to the flames without being singed in the process.

I'd have welcomed the risk, but the choice isn't mine to make.

I let out a deep sigh and stare up at the starry night sky. "V, I'm gonna take a walk, okay? I'll see you in the morning."

He lifts an eyebrow at me, a clear sign that he thinks I'm a complete idiot for appearing in public, at night, and by myself after three attempts were made on my life only days earlier. He's probably right, but it won't stop me from living.

Besides, if some other jackass takes a shot, maybe this time I'll be smart about it and get a name before killing him.

Vittorio finally nods at me before heading inside the lobby. "I'll have a team here waiting, just in case."

"Thanks."

I watch him disappear beyond the front doors and then jog down a set of steps heading toward the Mediterranean. I pull off my shoes and socks once I step onto the sand, the crunch of the grains between my toes putting me at ease. I let the salty air fill my lungs and the soft ripple of the crashing waves infuse my senses.

Part of the reason why I chose this place was because of its proximity to the sea. How ironic that the waves that tossed and tussled my young body around to the point that CPR almost didn't restart my heart are the only bit of peace and tranquility I have in my life right now?

I don't ever wander back into those waters...I haven't since that almost-fateful day. Instead, I just watch and admire. On the surface, the sea is so beautiful. Vibrant and breathtaking, yet at the same time so turbulent and volatile.

It has the power and potential to bring complete and utter chaos to someone's life in the blink of an eye.

Much like me.

It reminds me of the destruction that can be caused at my hand if I make the wrong move.

Or the right one.

I can't always tell the difference.

I walk closer to the packed wet sand where the waves rush forward, dragging pebbles, shells, and sediment onto the shore. I dig in my toes, wiggling them in the cool grains, but careful not to let the water touch me.

I back away as the next wave crashes, the spray splashing in all directions. A muffled cry from a few feet away startles me, and I twist around in the darkness, my hand on the gun tucked into the waistband of my tuxedo pants.

A dark, hunched-over figure sits alone on the sand, tracing something with a long stick. If I strain my ears, I can hear snippets of a one-sided conversation. I watch for a minute, squinting to get a clearer view.

That's when her head tilts toward the moonlit sky. She raises her eyes to the heavens, tears glistening on her cheeks. Her hair cascades over her quivering shoulders as the sob explodes from her chest. She drops the stick and covers her face with her hands.

Natalya.

My chest tightens and at once, I forget about why I'm out here, about who's looking for me, and about how I'm going to survive the next attempt on my life.

All I can wonder about is her.

Is she working with my enemies?

Or is she one of them?

Don't do it, Cristian. There are too many risks...to you, to your family. You have an obligation to them.

That knowledge doesn't stop my feet from walking toward her, though.

And it's not because I have the burning need to comfort her.

There are other burning needs consuming me like wildfire right now and seeing her so broken makes me want so much more than just a little taste.

I want to devour her like she's my last meal on Earth.

Consequences be damned.

I close the distance between us, dropping to my knees when I'm mere inches away. She looks up with a loud gasp, clutching her chest.

"Relax," I say, putting a hand on her arm. "It's me."

Tears flow faster from her eyes. "Oh, just great. The one person I want to see right now." Even through her sorrow, sarcasm laces her words.

"My presence doesn't usually accompany tears." I smirk. "At least, when I show up on the scene. They usually come after I leave."

She rolls her eyes, wiping her eyes with the sleeve of her sweatshirt. "You're unbelievable, do you know that?"

"That's what I hear." I nod at the spot next to her. "Mind if I sit?"

"I don't own the beach. But you probably can since you're such great friends with that scumbag Michel Dubois. I'm sure he'll give you a good price."

I sink into the sand, turning to look at her. I fight every urge to fling my body on top of hers and fuck her until she can't remember that cocksucker's name.

Because he's not worth the tears.

And the something she wants is the one thing I can give her.

Maybe it'll get me in her good graces.

Maybe it'll get me close to Alek.

Maybe it'll get me to a place where I can finally get some answers.

But most importantly, it might make her look at me a little differently, like I'm *not* a cockroach wandering around her kitchen.

"From what I hear, your father was a pretty powerful force here when he was alive."

"Yeah, that's what I hear, too," she grumbles. "Not that it's done me a damn bit of good."

"You know how things work. You have to prove your worth to the people in charge if you want their help."

"I figured I'd get their help because of who I am and what my family has done for this place."

"They only care about money. If their sources of income dry up… which they kind of did when your dad died…then just a name alone isn't going to get them excited."

"It's just been hard." She sniffles. "I thought coming here would be a good move for me, and now I just hate it. Everything it represents. But I—I just wanted to feel closer to my father. I know, it probably sounds stupid. But he loved it here. Loved his hotels. And the one I'm running was one of his passion projects. That's why I came. I wanted to make sure I carried out his vision." She lets out a dry laugh. "And it's destroying me. This place, the people, the memories. All of it. It's toxic." With the sweep of her hand, she pushes back her hair. Her fresh, clean scent intoxicates me, and I need to remind myself to focus on my objective.

Not how good she smells.

"I don't even know why I told you all of that." She digs her toe into the sand. "You're an asshole who's trying to torpedo my hotel." With a harsh glare, she pins me to the spot. "Do you want to know why I wanted that land so badly?"

I'm honestly too stunned to speak. Natalya is unraveling right before my eyes, and I swear, I've never seen anything sexier. She's got the tongue of a viper, but her vulnerability shocks the shit out of me. I never saw it coming.

It makes me feel like I need to protect her.

And I want to protect her.

"Tell me," I murmur.

"Before he died, my dad wanted to build a brand-new restaurant, one he'd have one of the big celebrity chefs operate. He loved to cook a big dinner with my mom every Sunday before she died. It was really cute. It made us feel…"

She shrugs and stares out at the sea. "Normal, I guess. Once a week, things were calm. Happy. Not like anything else about our lives ever came close to normal. But the cooking made us feel safe and comfortable. It was our fun family day every week. No matter what Dad was doing the rest of the week, Sunday was ours. Together. Always."

I nod, rubbing the back of my neck. "And that's why you were so focused on getting rights to the land."

"Yeah, until you came along and screwed me over." Her shoulders hunch a bit lower. "And I pretty much just guaranteed that Dubois isn't going to help me do a goddamn thing while I'm here."

"Why? What happened?"

She peeks at me, the hint of a smile on her face. "I might have snapped his wrist tonight at the gala."

"Might have?"

She nods. "Yeah, and then I might have kneed him in the balls right afterward to make sure he really got the message."

I snicker. "Yeah, you're definitely fucked now."

She covers her face with her hands and lets out a loud groan. "I don't know what the hell I was thinking. Actually, I wasn't thinking at all. I'm blaming the vodka."

"And what about now? Am I starting to break you down? Or is it still the vodka that's keeping you around?"

"Well, it's made me tired enough that I don't feel like walking back up to the hotel." Tali chuckles, flinging herself back onto the sand.

"With all of the booze you put away tonight, I'm surprised you could still walk all the way down here."

She peers up at me. "I'm Russian. It's in my blood, just like wine and olive oil run through *your* veins, goombah."

"Touché, Red Square." I pull off my tie and unbutton the top of my shirt. I really hate being in suits.

She giggles, stretching her arms overhead. "I think I'm going to stay right here tonight. I'm not going to make it back up the beach. My legs are done working today."

"Won't your boyfriend miss you?" I don't even know where the hell that came from.

"I don't really care. I won't miss *him*."

"I bet he'd come looking for you." I take a breath. "I would."

She gazes up at me, and I know I'm damn close to crossing a line.

Don't go there, Cristian. You might not make it back...

I can hear Jak in my ear, but all of his warnings just fade to the background like white noise.

Or the waves crashing onto the shore.

I silently will Jak to shut the fuck up.

I don't even know if there is a line to cross.

Christ, all I needed to do was get close to her, to find out if she knows anything I can use. And here I am sitting next to her on a beach, thinking of all the ways I can make her scream and writhe and beg for my cock.

To say I've failed in my quest is a fucking understatement.

"Why'd you come here?" Tali asks.

I stare out at the sea. "I needed to think. And get away from all of the shit that plagues me every day. I like being here on the beach. Helps me clear my head."

"And what about Monaco? Why did you put up that hotel? Aren't you supposed to be some shipping titan? That's what your family is known for, right? Transporting...*olive oil*?"

"My dad was the titan. But, ah...he's gone now."

She sits straight up. "I'm sorry. I didn't know."

"Yeah, it happened a couple of months ago. You're not the only one who knew about the shipping business. It's huge. Worth billions." I pick up the stick she'd been playing with earlier and trace a pattern in the sand. "But there are people who didn't like him being in control of so much wealth. So they decided to go after it. And him."

Tali shakes her head. "It must have been really hard on you. Do you have family?"

"My mom died when I was little, but yeah, I have four brothers and a sister. Most of them are back in Sicily. One of my brothers is here with me."

"So why are you here, then?" Her eyebrows furrow. "Shouldn't you be home with your family? Figuring out your next step? Trying to hold onto the shipping business?"

Her line of questioning doesn't give me a goddamn thing. If she didn't even know Dad was killed...and no, I don't think she's that great of an actress to have pretended she didn't...then how the hell could she possibly know anything about Daniel Tava? Or the hit on me the other night?

The only thing I do know is that she's upset. Sad about her own dad. Having to deal with me and the rest of the corrupt assholes who run this place.

She isn't involved. She can't be.

If anyone knows anything, it would be her brother, Alek.

And if he feels about his sister the way I feel about mine, he'd never let her in on anything that could possibly hurt her.

I need to get to Alek. He'd be the one with the answers.

Not Tali.

"We're trying to figure out how to put the pieces back together, I guess." I look at her. "Just like you. New opportunities, ways to expand. If people are targeting our biggest money-maker, maybe we need to build more. Do different things."

"Makes sense," she muses, sweeping her hand through the cool sand and letting it fall from her fingertips. "This was my dad's favorite place in the world. He loved living here. He found a lot of peace here after my mom died. Me, I'm still searching for that peace."

"Why are you having such a hard time?" I can't help but ask the question. Or maybe I want to keep her talking because it's the longest stretch of time we've been together without me pissing her off enough to send her stalking in the other direction. For some reason, she's staying right here.

With me.

And that's exactly where I want her to be.

She rubs her eyes. "Because of the way things happened. My mom died in a brutal attack. I'd been targeted, too. And it was because of me that we were in the line of fire. I was being my typical bitchy self, and I made her take me out to the mall when we both knew it wasn't safe. I escaped. She didn't. And then when my dad..."

Tali pauses, shaking her head. "It shouldn't have happened. He shouldn't have died. If I'd have been there, maybe I could have helped him."

"Or maybe you might have gotten killed yourself."

"Maybe. It doesn't make me feel any better. The only thing that makes me feel a tiny bit better, a tiny bit closer to him, is being here. That's why I came. And I feel like it was a really huge mistake. I was stupid for leaving Las Vegas." She looks up at me, her voice a soft whisper. "I don't even know why I'm telling you any of this. I hate you."

"Do you really?"

"I think so, yes."

"You don't seem like you want to impale me with a shoe right now. Maybe I am wearing you down after all? Maybe my charm is finally working?"

"Or maybe it's like I said before. My legs don't work, and I can't get up and run away from you."

"Maybe it's because you don't really want to go."

We stare at each other for what feels like hours. I can see a heaviness in her crystal blue eyes. It's the same one I carry around deep in my heart. We're both searching for answers, wondering what the future holds for us, trying to figure out how to move on from the demons lurking in all corners of this life we lead.

Because it's really the same life.

With the same dangers looming.

Wrought with the same heartache.

I watch her watching me. Her hair is splayed out on the sand beneath her head, but she doesn't seem to care about the grit against her scalp. The deep vee neck of her t-shirt gives a hint of what lies beneath the fabric, the perfect tits that I've longed to taste ever since I saw them peeking out of her gown earlier tonight. The smooth column of her neck beckons my lips, and I have to ball my fists to keep my fingers under control when all they want to do is touch and tug and taunt.

Dammit, it's hard to stare and not fantasize about what could be...

What could have been if things were different.

I still have a chance to make it all better. Maybe not for myself, but at least for her.

"I want you to have the land."

She blinks fast, an expression of confusion flitting across her face. "I don't understand. You tried so hard to snag it right out from under me. Why would you give it up so easily?"

Somehow telling her that I only wanted to see if I could buy the protection I need from the government doesn't seem like a great move.

And besides, I have zero faith that my new friend Michel Dubois can do a goddamn thing to help me.

I'm on my own.

Like I always am.

"You have plans." I shrug. "Take it. Make your dad's dream a reality. Finish the passion project."

Tali rolls onto her side, her eyes narrowed. "And what do you want in return?"

"Nothing." And I don't. Not for the land, anyway.

"So you're just going to sign over the rights and walk away from it? From your top competitor?"

"I already told you, your clientele isn't my target." I snicker. "Your hotel is better suited to the commoners."

She gasps and flings a fistful of sand at me. "You asshole! It is not!"

I roll to my feet and grab my own handful of sand, tossing it at her head.

With a loud giggle, she jumps up, kicking sand in my direction as she chases me to the shore. I run backward so I can keep an eye on her and the wide smile plastered across her face.

I don't think I've ever seen it before.

It shines so bright, it rivals the moonlight.

The sand gets cooler and wetter beneath my feet, but I keep moving. She is running at top speed until her foot gets caught in a hole a few inches from the shore, making her lose her balance. Tali topples forward, leaping at me to steady herself.

I fall back onto the packed sand, Tali landing cleanly on top of me. Her long, soft hair drapes over my chest as she pushes herself up, her soft laugh making my heart hammer hard and fast. Everything about this woman completely captivates me. She makes me think things I shouldn't, want to do things I know are wrong. Her presence consumes me, making everything else fade into the air around us.

And it isn't until the frigid wave crashes over us that I realize I'm in the water, and for the first time since my near-death experience, I'm not afraid.

I'm calm.

Because of her.

When did I become *that* guy?

Her chest heaves on top of me, her fingers clutching the sides of my shirt. Tiny drops of water cling to her cheeks, but that smile...it never fades. It's exactly as I'd imagined.

I never want to be the reason why it disappears from her face.

My arms are wrapped around her from when she tumbled into me, and I don't want to let her go.

She belongs to someone else, Cristian.

It's too risky. You need to stay away.

I'm tired of hearing those voices taunt me.

I know what I need to do.

I know I have to walk away.

I know a lot of things.

But for as much as I know, I feel even more.

I don't know how I let this happen.

I had two jobs to do—find Dad's killer and figure out who murdered Daniel Tava.

It's been two months, and I have nothing except a raging hard-on for a woman who's family might be involved.

Chapter Eleven
CRISTIAN

My arms tighten around Tali, and her lips part, her head leaning toward me as if she's in a trance and unable to break free from my hold on her.

Maybe she doesn't even want to try.

I can practically taste her, she's so close.

"Don't," I rasp, my throat so tight I can barely choke out the single word. Because my body and mind are definitely in the *do* camp. And I know that if her perfect pink lips graze mine, I won't be able to stop myself from carrying out each and every fantasy that's been looping through my mind.

"Oh, my God." Pushing herself off of me, she recoils and falls back onto the sand, swinging herself up to a sitting position. "Oh, my God! What the hell is wrong with me? I...I can't believe I just...with *you*..." She groans and jumps to her feet. "So stupid. I am so fucking stupid! I never learn!"

I stand up, inching toward her as she sways slightly in the sand. I let out a deep sigh. "Tali, it's just not the right time. For either of us. You're upset. And drunk. And I can't take advantage of that. I won't."

She pokes me in the chest, her teeth clenched. "You've been feeding me lines and innuendoes since the first time we met! I actually listened to all of your bullshit. I bought it! And tonight, I actually thought it might be real!" She looks at me, her eyes glittering with a whole mess of emotions—disgust, embarrassment, fury, pain. They're all festering in that heated gaze. I wish I could erase them all, look into her eyes, and just see hope.

For once.

I want to know it's there and that deep down, she has it.

I know I do.

"It was real. *Is* real." I look away before hammering the final nail in the coffin. "But it's not enough. Besides, there's the boyfriend. I'm not a homewrecker."

Her eyes widen. "The boy—fuck," She backs away from me, turns, and runs toward the stairs leading to her resort.

"Tali!" I run after her, my feet pounding the sand as the grains get finer and less packed up the beach. It was easier to run near the damn water.

She gets to the hand rail by the first step and stops, her shoulders quaking, her breaths coming in pants. "Just leave me alone. I'm not enough for you, remember? I did hear that right, didn't I?"

I groan, holding the side of my head. Why the fuck can't I just escape my life for one goddamn night and give in to what I want most? "I didn't say you're not enough. I said *it's* not enough!"

"Well, what the hell is *it*?" she shrieks, fisting her sand-crus hair. "No, wait, you know what? I don't give a shit! Okay? S can just go and fuck *yourself* tonight, how about that?"

"Tali, I'm not letting you walk back alone." I grab her wrist and look around at the desolate beach.

"I told you not to call me that!" she yells, pulling her wrist out of my loose grip.

"Fine. *Natalya*. Your hotel was bombed the other day. Who the hell knows who might be out there watching?"

She lets out a sharp laugh. "Bombed. Yeah. That's right. I'm under attack. From the whole goddamn world!"

I wasn't sure before, but now I'm convinced she's way more hammered than she let on. "It's not safe," I murmur. "Let me walk you back."

Her eyes flash with a murderous glare. "No," she hisses. "Because you're right. *Anybody* can be watching."

I watch her stagger up the stairs and disappear at the top of the staircase. I wait a minute, then run up the stairs behind her. She may not want me to walk her back, but she can't control which route I take back to my own place. I keep enough of a distance that nobody looking would think we're walking together, but I can close the space between us in a hot second if I need to.

I adjust my pants as I creep along behind her. My dick is not happy right now.

Hell, the rest of me isn't exactly jumping for joy, either.

A few minutes later, she disappears into the back entrance of her resort. I let out a deep breath and lean against a nearby palm tree and let the voices in my head rage.

She was drunk. And angry. And depressed. You did the right thing. You were a gentleman and you didn't take advantage of her.

Gentleman, my ass. She could be riding me like a fucking horse jockey right now!

I clutch the sides of my head as I walk back to my own hotel. My temples are pounding, and I need an ice cold shower to wash away the lust clouding my mind. The deep ache in my balls tells me that it's gonna be a long night.

A long, *lonely* night.

I wander through the gardens lining the perimeter of my hotel, following the path around trees and bushes surrounding the building. A rustling of leaves makes me jump, until I realize the sea breeze has picked up force. I rake a hand through my hair. "I need to get my head on straight," I grumble. "And remember why I'm in this damn place." I round a darkened corner and stop before taking another step. A shadow moves along the ground, the figure hidden behind a tall hedge.

Fuck.

Someone is always watching...

I crouch down, inching closer to the side of the hedge, silently berating myself for not grabbing a gun before I ventured onto the beach. Or a knife. Or even a fucking pen.

Anything that could save my ass right about now.

I creep forward until a gray ball of fur leaps past me.

"Meow!"

"Sonofabitch." I let out the breath I'd been holding. A cat. My eyes start tearing almost immediately since I'm deathly allergic to them. "Alright, get out of here before you take one of *my* nine fucking lives."

The cat looks up at me with bright yellow eyes, and I swear they roll upward before it turns and trots toward the beach.

I straighten up and scoff. "Even a stray cat can see how pathetic I—"

My head jerks back, forcing my back to arch. I yelp, swinging my arms around my back at whoever is now dragging me into the darkness. I dig my heels into the grass to give myself leverage and thrust my upper body forward with as much force as I can muster, flipping my assailant over my head. He crashes to the ground with a loud thump and a groan. I jump on top of him and pound my fist into his face over and over until his eyes are swollen shut and his mouth is gurgling blood.

The steel knife clutched in his hand now gleams on the grass a few feet away. As battered as he is, he still makes an attempt to grab it. I stomp on his hand before grabbing it myself and holding it up to his neck.

Get a name, you asshole!

"You guys are supposed to be killers?" I pant, my hand shaking. "You couldn't hit a target if someone smacked you in the fucking head with it! Now who are you working for?"

The man mutters something in French and I roll my eyes. "Christ, of course, you're French. You guys do better with cheese and croissants. You should stick to what you know." I press the knife deeper into his skin and a dot of blood appears. I yank him up by his hair. "Tell me now!" I growl against his ear.

"Fuck you," he grunts in a heavy accent.

"Sacré bleu!" I say in a mock French accent. "You mean you're not going to tell me who put the hit on me? You really want to die a slow and painful death?"

"Kill me. I don't give a shit. You won't survive the night. I'm not the only one looking for you."

I grip his hair tighter and press the knife into his throat. The dot of blood has turned into a thin trickle. "I'm not fucking kidding here, Pierre. Tell me who you're working—"

A searing pain explodes into my right shoulder where the shot tears through my flesh. The force throws me backward, clutching my arm. "Motherfucker!" I roll over onto my good shoulder, scrambling to my feet before another shot hits me somewhere else...a place I might not be able to recover from so quickly. Two more muted shots ricochet off the trunk of a tree next to me and I tear through an opening in the hedges, forgetting about the guy whom I'd been ready to gut only seconds earlier.

They were smart this time. Silencers.

I dig around in my pocket for my phone. Christ, did it fall out when I was on the beach?

I have nothing.

No fucking weapon, no way to get backup.

Sonofabitch!

This is *not* the way I planned to end my night.

The footsteps are getting closer, and I'm stuck in the middle of the fucking botanical gardens. My eyes dart left and right. They're coming. At least two of them, if not more.

I press my spine to the stone wall and wait.

It won't be long.

Five, four, three—

The footsteps get louder and heavier as they rush into the garden. I don't think, I just attack. An elbow to the temple and a kill punch to the throat and motherfucker number one drops his gun. I grab it and fire off two shots to the head. Motherfucker number two drops to the ground like an anchor hitting the bottom of the ocean.

But motherfucker number three is a little more skilled than his dead pals. He drives his elbow down on my outstretched one before I can squeeze off a shot. The force loosens my grip and the gun crashes to the ground. I don't stop, though. I crouch low, diving at his feet. He crashes into a bush behind him, firing a shot into the air and missing me entirely.

Eight lives left, Cristian...

I drive my fist into his gut, over and over until he kicks me away from him. He jumps out of the bush, landing cleanly on the ground, and points the gun at me.

Crack! Crack! Crack!

His body shudders as the bullets pepper him from behind and he face-plants into the dirt. I drop to my knees and pull him up by the hair, then slam his head back to the ground.

I drag myself to my knees, pushing back my hair. "Thanks, man," I say to Vittorio when I see him emerge from a few feet away.

"I told you not to go down there by yourself," he grunts.

"I was fine down on the beach. Shit went sideways when I got back to the hotel. These assholes were coming for me. Inside, outside. They were gonna find me."

"Amateurs," he mutters, glaring at the three bodies. "Too stupid to know who they were dealing with."

"They never realize it," I say, still trying to catch my breath.

"What the fuck happened here?" Diego runs through the bushes, stopping short before stepping on one of the fucknuts who tried to take me out and failed pretty miserably.

"It's the after-party," Vittorio snarls.

Diego chuckles, clapping Vittorio on the shoulder. "Keep that sense of humor, V. I have a feeling you're gonna need it." He looks at me. "I don't suppose you're any closer to figuring out who the hell is so intent on killing you."

"Sorry," I groan, shifting my arm back. "I got shot right before I could get it out of them."

"Christ," Diego mutters, peering at my shoulder. "Let's get you upstairs. V, you can deal with this, yeah?" He motions to the bodies.

Vittorio grunts a reply. He doesn't ever really speak. It's always more guttural with him. He's a badass mother in every way, six foot eight and three-hundred-and-fifty pounds. But he's stealth like a ninja and runs like a gazelle. He's also a perfect shot. That shit makes him invaluable to us.

Diego pulls my good arm toward one of the entrances to the hotel. I hand him a key and he sticks it into the lock, twisting it and shoving me inside.

"Jesus, why don't you just throw me through the glass? Why bother unlocking the door?" I groan, holding my arm.

"Listen, dumbass. You don't know if there are more guys out there waiting to pounce. Someone wants you dead. Like, yesterday. Show your face outside again, and who the hell knows what will happen?"

"So I'm just supposed to sit inside and cower while Dad and Daniel's killer stalk me? They're not just looking for me, Diego. Remember? You're on their hit list, too."

"They seem to be putting a lot more effort into nailing you than me."

"It's because they think you're an idiot who just thinks with his dick," I grumble. "Nobody is scared of you because they think your brain is in the head of your cock, which is usually buried inside some bleached blonde whore."

"Hey, hey. I love brunettes, too. And like I told you before, it makes me dangerous. They never see me coming." Diego knocks on the doctor's door. He answers pretty quickly, and we walk into the room where he has his own private emergency room already set up.

And even though putting him up here at the hotel costs me plenty, it's a necessary expense.

I think I've made back my investment on it in the past couple of days alone.

Doc raises an eyebrow as he looks at my shoulder. "No exit wound. This is gonna take me awhile."

He gets started right away, digging around in my flesh for the bullet. The searing pain is excruciating and it explodes down the length of my arm. He finally pulls it out with a pair of tweezers and holds it up in front of me.

"Thank Christ," I grunt through clenched teeth. "Tell me I can have some scotch now, Doc."

"Not quite yet," Doc says, prepping his needle so he can sew me back up. "You know the drill."

Diego studies his phone but stays silent. I know that won't last too long. We never talk business in front of Doc. He only knows what he knows so we make sure that isn't much.

I trust him to put me back together when I'm broken, but it's better that he doesn't have too many details.

It keeps us all safer.

I grip the table as each stitch pulls the sides of my wound together, swallowing the colorful expletives and death threats hanging on the tip of my tongue. Doc works without speaking, so there are no bullshit pleasantries to exchange. I suffer with each tug and pull of the needle and surgical thread until he finally finishes.

He looks at me. "You know how it works. Move around too much and the stitches will split. Keep yourself in check and you'll heal no problem."

Diego winks at me. "Think you can handle that? Or are you gonna disregard the doctor's orders completely?"

I roll my eyes. "Let's see what tomorrow brings." I can see the Doc's face twist into a grimace.

"He knows I'll be here waiting for the replay," the Doc says, throwing up his hands.

"I like to keep you sharp," I say, clapping Doc on the back with my good hand. "Thanks. Beautiful work, as usual."

"Let's hope it lasts more than a few hours."

Diego follows me out of the room, closing the door tight behind us.

We don't speak until we're back in my apartment. I'm not sure why. This hotel doesn't house anyone besides us, the Doc, and our security. But still, we save the business talk for when we're behind closed doors.

And once they close, all hell breaks loose.

"How many more times do you think you can escape whoever is after you?" Diego bellows at me, pouring my best scotch into two highball glasses.

I collapse onto my couch, leaning my head back against the leather cushion. "Infinity."

"They gunned down Dad in cold blood and took out Daniel Tava, making it look like an accident. They were the two heads of the biggest shipping business in Europe. I don't have to remind you that it's more than just a simple coincidence, do I? These people are out for blood—Marcone blood, obviously—and our money. This is the second time they've come at you, and we still have no leads on who we're dealing with. They won't stop until they get you. Until they get everything."

"They're a bunch of hacks. Couldn't assassinate me if they had a loaded gun at my temple and I was tied to the back of a chair." I wince, shifting onto my good side. "Besides, Jak already read me the riot act tonight at the gala."

"It doesn't seem to have done much good since you still went down to the beach by yourself like a complete ass."

"I wasn't by myself."

Diego looks up and hands me a glass. "Vittorio said you went alone."

"Yeah, I did go alone."

"Did you meet somebody out there?"

"Nah, I already knew who she was."

Diego's eyes narrow. "Cristian, what happened down there?"

"Natalya Severinov was on the beach."

"Jesus," Diego mutters before taking a long gulp of scotch. "What the hell went on? Don't tell me you—"

"I didn't," I say in a flat voice. "But not because I couldn't have. She was all in. But I know the rules…and the risks. So I turned her down."

Diego springs up from the couch. "Lemme get this straight. You were with *her*, the infamous Russian mafia princess who is desperate to grab her slice of the Severinov family pie and turn it into her own empire since she no longer has her dad to do it for her and she wants to be taken seriously."

"That was a lot of exposition. I didn't realize you were such an expert on their family."

"You were with her. She tried to come on to you and you rejected her. Like actually told her no?"

"Basically."

"And then what happened?"

"She left. Walked back to her hotel alone."

"And you let her go?"

"She insisted."

"So then you came back here by yourself and almost got massacred."

I hold up a hand. "Easy. It was more like a bunch of frat guys playing paintball. Hardly the makings of a massacre. And I got most of them."

"If Vittorio hadn't shown up, your ass would have been terminated."

"Just my ass?"

"Well, yeah, although lately your ass has become more of a hat since your head is shoved so far up inside of it."

"Thanks."

"Just making an observation." Diego sighs and rotates his glass. "Here's another one for you. It's very possible the Severinov family had something to do with these killings."

I press an ice pack against my shoulder. "Jak said the same thing."

Diego nods. "Smart guy."

"I don't think so, though."

"Based on what? The fact that you've got a hard-on for Natalya? Because that's never come back to bite you, right? Mixing business and pleasure?"

"Look, nothing happened between us." I close my eyes, an image of her smiling face floating into my mind. It actually takes away the pain for a second. Better than any drug.

"But you like her. I saw you together at the gala. Just because *you* don't think anyone is watching doesn't mean that's the case."

And then the pain is back, like a continuous stabbing sensation. It makes my entire arm throb, just like my head is doing from Diego's third degree. "Did you know that the Severinovs work with a company out of Albania that owns a good number of ports along the same waterways? Don't you think they'd be interested in getting a piece of our shipping territories? So they don't have to pay the Albanians and can move their shit around freely?"

"You're saying they're just going to kill everyone in their way to cut out the middleman?" I shake my head. "I don't get that vibe from them."

"Listen, I know you think you know her, but—"

"Trust me, Diego. She has her own problems. Lots of them, one of which happens to be that her own hotel was bombed the other day. Remember? The Severinov family has enemies right here whom they need to deal with. I just don't think they're involved."

Diego springs up from his seat on the couch. "Let me break this down for you so you actually get my point since the painkillers are clearly rotting away your brain." I can tell from the tone of his voice that he's about to start pacing, and he doesn't disappoint. I'd roll my eyes if it didn't hurt so much.

Everything hurts.

I just want to sleep.

I try to focus, but my eyes are heavy.

He'd better make this fast. And clear. I don't know how much longer I have.

I sit as straight as I can, hoping it'll make me pay closer attention to my brother's explanation.

"She lured you down to the beach, Cristian! She had it all planned out!"

Here we go. I groan, holding my arm. "She didn't even know I'd be there. She was alone when I found her."

"But she left you behind and went back to her place alone. It's not hard to put an attack together if everyone is in place and ready to pounce."

"I could have fucked her on the beach. Then she wouldn't have run away."

"Unless someone went looking for her."

"I'm not really impressed with any of these theories, Diego," I say with a loud yawn. "Even all drugged up, I can shoot 'em down. Every one."

"The Severinovs need to be on your radar." Diego narrows his eyes at me. "Don't you go thinking with your dick now."

"Works for you, doesn't it?"

"If you think I'm so off-base, get to Alek Severinov. Feel him out, see what he knows."

"You really think he's just gonna tell me if he's trying to kill me? And the rest of our family?"

"I think if you talk to him, you might get some answers. Remember, we need to find the people responsible. I'm not saying the

Severinovs put the hit out, but maybe they know who did. Maybe they're working with the people who did because they were given a pretty big incentive to take us out of the equation, like a piece of our shipping business."

"I barely know the guy. I'm supposed to sit down with him, shoot the shit, and then ask if he knows who's trying to kill me?"

"Basically. If you catch him off-guard, he might give a tell. From what I know, Alek is trying to keep his family's interests from going up in flames, so if anyone approached him with an opportunity, I think he'd take it. And he's got no loyalty to us."

"What about the bomb at Natalya's hotel? Doesn't that tell you they have their own enemies to battle? And if you're right about their 'interests,' then the same people who are after us might be after them, too, especially if they're the 'competition' for those ports?"

Diego narrows his eyes, quiet for a second. Not nearly long enough, if you ask me. He finally nods, I guess to acknowledge that my theory is a damn good one...and one he didn't think of himself. How about that for being doped up on painkillers? "You make a good point, although I still think mine is better. Just remember that anything is possible. And if the Severinovs are being targeted, too, then maybe it's a good idea for us to band together. Take out whomever we need."

"So...I have to go find Alek..." My voice trails off, my head slumping to the left against the couch cushion. The ice pack falls to the floor. I've done enough thinking for tonight. My mind is on low power mode right now.

"Yeah, you do." Diego pulls me up from the couch, leading me into my bedroom.

"I'm tired right now." My eyes droop closed, and he guides me through the doorway, slamming my good arm into a wall. "You fucking ass..." I say, my words slow and slurred.

"That was for challenging my brilliant theory," he replies with a snicker.

He lowers my body to the bed, hoisting me up with pillows. I collapse backward and a chill settles onto my shoulder when Diego puts the ice pack on top of my wound.

I drift off to sleep, the memory of Tali stretched out on top of me flashing behind my closed eyes. The way her body felt plastered against mine, the scent of her perfume, the desire glittering in the depths of her bright blue eyes.

God, I wanted to taste those lips.

I really hope she isn't the one trying to kill me so I actually get that chance.

Chapter Twelve
TALI

Blinding white light burns my tear-filled eyes. I clutch the side of my head, the impact making my temples throb. My fingertips feel wet and the spot on my skin stings when I press them to it. I yelp when I pull them away and see that they're stained a bright red.

My teeth chatter uncontrollably as I try to catch my breath.

I turn toward Alain who is gripping the steering wheel of my car...the car that I couldn't drive because I'd had way too much champagne after seeing the latest tabloid eruption come to life, starring none other than my boyfriend.

He'd been cozying up to some C-list actress from America in a corner at a party we'd just left. Did he really think I wouldn't notice? Or maybe that I'd be too drunk to care?

It took everything in me not to pull her away by her long blonde hair extensions and snap his neck on the spot.

It was over in that second.

We were over.

Carrying on behind my back was one thing, but doing it out in the open?

Done and done.

I needed a distraction because I was lonely.

He was it.

But I'm past all of that.

Or am I?

I swallow the sob rising in my throat, gripping the dashboard.

He reaches out and yanks my face toward him, his eyes black beads filled with evil, his words dripping with malice. "I own you, Tali. So cry as much as you want now, but tomorrow, remember this. Your life is mine."

The nightmare that torments me, whether or not my eyes are closed, is once again on repeat.

I'd hoped that something would have replaced those horrific images and sounds last night, the ones that loop through my sleep-induced mind every time I fall into my bed. But no.

Cristian forced me away.

He was the one person who could have soothed my tortured soul and given me some peace.

Even if only for a few hours.

I lean over the balcony in my bedroom, breathing in the sea air. It doesn't smell nearly as sweet as it did last night when I'd crashed into Cristian on the beach. For those few minutes, I felt free…freer than I have in weeks.

I opened up to him in a way I swore I'd never do again after my experiences with that asshole Alain. I told him things I haven't shared with anyone. Not even Kaz, my twin and the closest person to me in the world.

I fanned out all of my cards, showing Cristian my hand with no hesitation.

But he passed on it.

He passed! He sent me away!

I practically threw myself at him and he pushed me aside.

Because he, like all other men, is completely full of shit.

I'd like to say I finally learned my lesson, but let's be real.

I fell for the lines.

And the panty-melting smile.

And the eyes I thought I could happily drown in.

I shared my deepest thoughts because I thought he cared.

Because I needed someone to talk to, someone to just listen without passing judgment.

We're the same, him and I.

The same, but so freaking different.

A loud knock at my door jolts me from the poisonous thoughts flying through my mind about what I'd like to do to Mr. Marcone if I ever see him again. The limbs I'd like to tear off of his body, the hair I'd like to yank from his scalp, the soft lips I'd love to nibble...

Oh, damn, my traitorous mind went there.

No! He doesn't get the pleasure of feeling my mouth anywhere near his!

Dammit. Hot mess express, pulling into the station...*now*!

I run toward the door and pull it open. My chest tightens, and I swear a sharp pain shoots down my left arm.

That smug bastard's knowing grin is enough to send me into panic attack mode.

Alain forces the door open wider so he can push past me.

Not that he needs the space.

Little pencil dick motherfucker.

He could worm his way into a room through a keyhole.

Ugh, what the hell was I thinking?

It's a choice that haunts me to this day.

"What do you want?" I look at him with every ounce of disgust that festers in my body, and fling my door closed so hard, the walls shake.

He pulls out his phone and shoves it in my face. "This doesn't look like part of our agreement, does it?"

I peer at the photo of me standing close to Cristian at the gala last night...and it's next to one of the two of us looking nice and cozy on the beach.

For a split second, I let my mind wander back to last night when his taut muscles tightened against me, when his heated gaze unraveled my inhibitions...

Argh!

And then when he let me go.

I grit my teeth. "So, it's fine for you to go parading around with your Eurotrash whores, but I'm not allowed the same freedom? I'm just supposed to sit here, letting you fuck every piece of ass all over the world with no response other than a smile?" I stick out my hand and push against his chest. "Au contraire, mon frère! Translation: Screw you, asshole! I'm not your goddamn doormat!"

"You'll be whatever I want you to be!" He puffs out his chest, his eyes blazing. "Do I need to remind you what's at stake if you open your mouth? Let me assure you it'll be much worse if you open your legs!"

"This..." I say through clenched teeth. "...is *over*! I will not be your prisoner anymore!"

Alain smiles and my insides go into deep-freeze mode. "Oh, Tali," he says, cupping my chin gently at first, then clutching it tight in his hand. "Don't be fucking stupid. You have a lot to protect. I certainly hope you didn't forget about it. You've already seen what I can do...how I can't get caught...do you think you have the same ability? Do you think you'll be safe? Do you think your brothers will be?" He points to his phone. "And your little fuck buddy. Do you think he has a shot in hell?" Alain shakes his head, his eyes spitting a combination of pure hate and rage. "None of you are safe. None of you are protected. And none of you will survive if you call any bit of attention to yourself like this again." He squeezes my chin, forcing me to look at him. Bile rises in my throat, and if I open my mouth, his Louis Vuitton suit will be covered in the manifestation of *my* hate and rage.

And just like that, he has me.

Because he knows very well that I have *nothing*.

He's seen my hand. Knows my tells.

I went all in with him.

And I never really made it out.

Judging from recent events, I don't know if I ever will.

I grab his wrist tight and fling him around my back so he slams into the back of the front door with a loud thud. His eyes widen, his wrist bent dangerously far back. I wish he'd seen what Michel Dubois looked like, doubled over and begging for mercy after *he* dared put his hands on me.

"Don't you ever fucking lay a finger on me again," I hiss. "I will snap your puny ass in two!"

His eyes bug and I smile, leaning close. "You didn't think I had it in me, did you? You thought I was some weak, pathetic bitch who couldn't handle anything on her own. So you swooped in and took control when I was grieving and at my lowest. And then you used it to exploit me, you cocksucker." I run my tongue over my lips. "Let's get this straight right now. You don't own me. You don't run my life. And you certainly don't tell me what to do, who to talk to, or who to fuck!" My voice roars in the expansive space, and a look of primal fear shadows Alain's face for a split second.

Good.

I want him to feel that kind of fear, the one that seeps into your bones and festers deep inside of you.

The fear I've lived with for the past weeks, waiting, wondering, and panicking about what comes next.

I don't know what it will be, but I will go down fighting until my last breath. I will defend everything important to me. I will yank back the control I allowed myself to give to him.

Because if I do none of these things, I'll just be a broken shell of my former self. A cracked, damaged shell with jagged edges and no soul.

I won't be that person anymore.

My life, my fucking way!

And I'll defend it, along with everything else I have to live for.

He won't strip away my control ever again.

"Do we understand each other?" I ask in a saccharin-sweet voice.

Honey...for the wasp.

He yanks back his wrist, but only because I loosen my grip enough for him to do so. My smile widens. "I don't think I heard your answer, Alain. Are we clear?"

He straightens up to his full height and puffs out his chest.

As if that's supposed to scare me.

Does he not realize the hell he has created for me over the past few weeks?

"I think you just made a very big mistake, Tali."

"Don't call me that," I seethe. "That nickname is reserved for friends. *We* are not friends. We are *nothing*."

"You're going to wish you hadn't made that choice, Natalya. You're going to wish for a lot of things in the very near future."

"You've been holding this over my head for too long, Alain. I'm prepared to deal with the consequences."

"Selfish bitch. Speaking on behalf of your brothers like that when you know very well what you stand to lose. What you *all* stand to lose when I go public with what you've done. People you didn't even know could be your enemies are waiting to punish the person responsible. You think I own you now? Just wait until they show up to collect what they're owed. You and your family won't stand a chance against them."

"If I have my family, I'm not worried about *you*. Or anyone else!" My hand closes around his neck and his face turns a disturbing shade of beet red. A smile plays at my lips. "You think you're the brain of your whole operation, but really, you're a message boy. If you had a real brain, you'd know who you're dealing with." I lean in, my nose practically touching his. "And you'd run the fuck away. As fast as your little Chanel loafers could carry you." I release him and his hands fly up to his neck. He sputters and spits, the color draining from his face.

I cock my head to the left. "By the way, I could have happily watched your eyeballs pop out of your skull a few seconds ago. Leave me and my family alone, or next time, I'll keep squeezing."

He lets out a sick and twisted laugh. It's almost demonic. "It doesn't matter what you do, Natalya. The evidence is stacked against you. There's no alibi that will free you. And that means your time is limited. Nowhere to run, nowhere to hide. You cost people a lot of money. They're coming, and I'm pointing them in your direction." He flashes a malicious grin. "You should have squeezed when you had the chance."

He pulls open the door, and with one final look of defeat, he slams it shut behind him.

I flip around, my back against the door. I slide to the floor, dropping my head into my hands.

I did what I set out to do. I pulled back the control, even for those few, triumphant minutes.

But did I really win?

Did I save myself and my family?

Or did I just dig myself into a deeper hole with no shot in hell for a lifeline?

Chapter Thirteen
CRISTIAN

The sun beats down on my back as I trudge down the road connecting my hotel to Tali's. Since my right shoulder was the one hit, I can't drive...my car, my bike. Vittorio offered to take me, but I'm not rolling in there in the back of some armored SUV.

If my enemies want me, they're going to have to come for me in the light of day. Mow me down, snipe me from a nearby building, jump out of a tree and slash my throat.

They can pick their poison.

I'm ready with mine.

I didn't tell Diego where I was going. He was too busy with an overnight guest who popped over after I'd passed out last night.

The drugs did me a lot of good. They erased the pain and kept the nightmares at bay.

But now it's morning and reality smacks me in the face.

Diego's arguments are valid. I can't ignore them.

It looks suspicious as hell, their family's involvement in the coastal territories now up for grabs, their need to re-establish themselves after their father died.

But deep down, I can't bring myself to believe that Tali had anything to do with that hit last night.

She's drowning in her own grief.

My chest tightens, her pained words and tears so vivid in my mind. All I wanted to do was take away the sadness, to soothe the ache deep in her heart.

To give her hope.

To make her smile.

So I did, at least for a few fleeting moments.

I can't shake the memory of the light in her eyes when she looked at me on the beach, the moonlight casting a glow over her head, the way her lips puckered when they were practically touching mine...

It couldn't have been bullshit.

It felt too real.

For a long time, I'd forgotten what *real* felt like, but last night, I remembered.

And then I pushed her away.

I walk up the driveway, sidestepping mopeds, cars, and people. I run a hand through my hair. Showering was a real bitch this morning, but at least my stitches are still intact. I didn't want to wear the sling Doc gave me.

Just another sign of weakness when what I need to portray is strength.

The wind flutters through the large plastic sheets lining the side of the lobby where the bomb had gone off only days earlier.

It feels like years have passed since then.

And judging from the way Tali worked her way around the gala last night, she's still searching for answers.

Just like I am.

I push through the revolving door and enter the lobby. I wander through the throngs of hotel guests, my temples pounding from a combination of the drills, saws, and ringing slot machines. I've never been inside here before, but I was lucky enough to get through to Alek Severinov this morning. After setting up a meeting, I asked how I could find Tali.

Surprisingly enough, he told me.

Diego would say it's another clue that she may be on board the Cristian killing train, especially after last night.

I mean, why else would Alek send me into the lion's den?

Anybody could be here hiding out, ready to strike at any second, especially if Alek alerted them that I'm on my way.

If they're the people who want me dead, I'm walking right into their trap.

But I don't care. I need to know if the Severinovs are part of the assassin team that can't get out of their own way and actually finish the job.

Another reason why I forgot to mention my little outing to Diego.

I have to do this alone, and I know he'd have had plenty of guys on my tail if he knew where I was going.

The private elevator that leads to Tali's apartment is hidden away in a corner of the lobby, off the casino floor. I stab the Up button and ride it to the top floor where Alek told me I could find Tali's apartment.

The elevator doors ping, and I step into the hallway. I'm consumed in white and cream accents, so bright, I almost have to shield my eyes. I take a few steps toward the doorway at the end of the hall and another door slightly to the right opens.

A tall, menacing-looking guy with dark hair and cold blue eyes steps out, his arms folded over his massive chest. I can definitely go toe to toe with this guy, but he has me on height. He's at least three inches taller than me.

Has he been waiting for me to show up?

Did Alek already pull the proverbial trigger?

A twinge in my shoulder reminds me that a tussle isn't exactly what the doctor ordered. I don't know who the fuck this guy is, but I need to figure out how to use my brain to get out of whatever awaits me as I get closer to Tali's door since I can't exactly use my body.

"So you're Cristian Marcone." The guy grunts as I stop in front of him.

"Yeah," I reply. "And you are?"

He smirks at me. "Kaz. Tali's brother. You scared yet?"

"Should I be?"

"If you're smart." He circles me like a lion eyeing a raw steak. "Why are you here to see my sister?"

"To finish a conversation."

"So, talking only?"

"Yep."

He nods his head at my shoulder. "Why's your arm so stiff?"

"I got shot last night."

"By who?"

"I don't know. I'd really like to find out."

"And you think she knows who it was?" His piercing eyes narrow to slits. "You here to get that information?"

"I'm actually hoping she doesn't know who it was."

We glare at each other, neither of us backing away, each of us holding our ground.

"Alek told me you were coming up."

"I figured."

"He doesn't trust you."

"Not surprising. I feel the same way about your family."

"Does Tali know you're coming?"

I shake my head. "Only if you guys told her."

He narrows his eyes at me. "I saw the pictures of you guys at the gala last night. Why are you sniffing out my sister? Don't you have enough of your own shit to handle without dragging her into it?"

"Seems like we both have a lot of shit to deal with, yeah?" I cock an eyebrow.

Kaz nods. "We do. I know all about your family—what you're into, what you're trying to salvage, who you're trying to escape from. But here's the deal, *friend*. I don't need your issues fucking with my family. Don't make my sister a target. You've got big problems with everyone in the world right now. Everyone wants a piece of you. And like you said, we have enough of our own shit to deal with. She was pretty rattled over that bomb. And with Daniel Tava being mowed down a couple of weeks ago..." He pushes against me, dipping his head to look down at me. "Nobody is safe."

But I don't move. My feet are rooted to the spot.

Daniel Tava. What the hell does he know about Daniel Tava?

An uneasy feeling makes my gut twist, and it's not because of Kaz flexing his biceps.

This guy is trying to intimidate me, and truth be told, he's pretty damn good at it.

Except I'm not one to be intimidated.

I'm here for answers.

And it seems that I have a hell of a lot more questions now.

"Like I said, I just want to finish a conversation."

"As you can see," Kaz says, cracking his knuckles. "I'm not really one for conversation."

"Lucky for me, it's your sister I want to talk to."

And the more this guy tries to muscle me, the more I think the Severinovs are not plotting against me after all. They have bigger fish to fry. I'm not sure what, but I make a mental note to have Jak look into it. If anything, we might be able to help each other.

But that's something I'll keep for my meeting with Alek.

If it turns out we're on the same team.

I'll know for sure when I see Tali...when I tell her—

The door creaks open, and Tali looks at me and her brother staring each other down in the middle of the hallway. "What the hell is going on out here?" Her head turns from me to Kaz and then back again. She glares at me. "You didn't say enough last night?"

Kaz's nostrils flare. "Tali, you want me to get rid of this guy? He says he's here to talk to you, but say the word and I'll make sure he never opens his mouth again because I'll wire it shut."

Goddammit, I wish I had full use of my shoulder. At least then it'd be a fair fight. I've heard of Kaz. He's one of the most deadly enforcers in the Russian mafia.

He'd make a worthy opponent, much better than the other jackasses who keep chasing their tails around, missing every chance to take me out.

I'm kind of caught between a rock and a hard place right now. If I go, I look like a pussy. If I stay, I may end up limbless.

All I want is five minutes with Tali.

I need to know what she's thinking…what she's feeling…if I blew my chance last night.

And if I'll get another one.

She lifts an eyebrow at me. "I was just going for a run, but I have a few minutes to talk."

"You sure?" Kaz asks, sneering at me. "You really want time alone with *The Godfather*?"

I roll my eyes, but keep my mouth shut. I need to be listening to any clues that can tell me who the hell is trying to exterminate me.

Her eyes flicker back to mine. Guarded again…is it because I fucked up by letting her walk away last night? "It's okay. *I'll* be okay."

Kaz nods at her and looks back at me. "Look, I know who you are and what you can do, Marcone, and I respect it. But the only reason why I'm letting this 'conversation' happen is because my sister can pull your nose through your asshole. And because she's sitting on an arsenal. Make a wrong move, and your shoulder will feel like a hangnail compared to what she'll do to you. And you'd better believe I'll be back to finish shit off."

"Noted," I grunt.

"When you're finished with this guy, text me. I'll make sure Leo and Myla are ready to head back to the airport. Unless we need to tie up any loose ends."

She nods, a small smile playing at her lips. "Thanks."

His grimace fades away and he winks at Tali. "Anything for my badass bitch of a sister." He pushes past me, nudging my bad shoulder.

What an asshole.

If it turns out they're behind this whole thing, I'm going after Kaz's ass first and I'm gonna annihilate it.

"Nice meeting you, too, dick," I mutter to his retreating back.

He flips me off before getting onto the elevator.

Tali leans back, opening the door for me. "How'd you even find me?"

"I called Alek."

"Great. I'll be sure to thank him later for giving me up like that." She folds her arms over her chest. "And why the hell would you be looking, anyway? Don't worry, I got your message loud and clear last night. I'm pretty swift, in case you didn't get that about me."

I lift my bad arm to sweep a hand through my hair, cringing as I realize my mistake. "Fuck!" I yelp, the pain exploding down my arm.

She furrows her brow. "What's wrong with your arm?"

"Someone tried to kill me last night when I was walking back to my hotel. Three someones, actually. One of them clipped me in the shoulder."

"Oh my God." Her jaw drops. "Wait, why would someone try to kill you? I mean, yeah, you're a cocky, sarcastic dickhead, but that's not really a sin that should be punishable by death. I'd think a severe ass-kicking would be much more in line with what you deserve." She cocks an eyebrow. "At least, after that shit you pulled with me."

"You don't forgive too easily, do you?"

"Forgive? Yeah, sure. I forgive. But I just never forget." She takes a step closer toward me. "Is that why you're here? You're looking for redemption before you meet your Maker so you can rest with a clear conscience?"

"I'd like to avoid meeting my Maker for a very fucking long time, especially if you're having second thoughts about trying to pull my nose through my asshole."

"Even if I was, what makes you think I'd make another offer? What makes you think you should get another chance?"

"Why'd you make the offer in the first place?"

"I had a bad night." She shrugs. "Followed by a lot of very bad months. Maybe you just caught me in a weak moment. A vodka-induced, very weak moment."

"Is that what you want me to believe? Or was there more behind it?"

"Why does it matter to you now? It didn't matter last night."

"Look, you were upset last night. And drunk. Much as you might not believe it, I'm not a complete asshole. I wouldn't have taken advantage of you like that, even if you stripped down naked on the beach."

There's a glimmer of something other than hate in her eyes.

Good. Maybe she isn't going to kill me after all. At least, right now.

But in a few seconds, who the hell knows what could happen?

So I take a gamble and keep going.

"I wasn't lying when I said things were complicated, Natalya."

"And they aren't now?"

"Oh no, things are worse now," I say, walking toward her slowly. "Seriously fucked up. To the point where I don't know which people I can trust, no matter how I feel about them."

Her eyes darken. "It's a bad place to be, isn't it?"

"It is. But it's not a place I want to stay in."

"Maybe you don't have a choice. Maybe someone else is making that decision for you. Maybe there isn't anything you can do to change your situation, even if you swear up and down that you will."

She turns her back on me and walks through the open sliding glass door where the balcony overlooks the waves of the Mediterranean crashing onto the shore.

I get the feeling we're not talking about me and my shitty predicament right now.

I wait for a few seconds and follow her outside, the balmy breeze whipping through my hair.

She turns toward me, her expression stony. "Sometimes you just can't make things right."

"What if you still want to try?"

"I don't know if it will matter. Some things just can't be salvaged. We all have to live with our choices, Cristian. And they will always come back to haunt us, even if we think we made the right ones." Tali shakes her head, a sorrow-filled expression clouding her perfect features.

"We're not talking about last night anymore, are we?" I ask.

She shakes her head. "You're not the only one running from your choices, Cristian. I really hope you can outlast yours. I'm not sure if I can outsmart my own." With a labored sigh, she tilts her head to the side. "Now tell me why you're really here, because I don't buy your forgiveness plea."

"Plea? I don't think I've begged for anything."

"Maybe not yet." A teasing smile lifts the corners of her lips, but it doesn't reach her eyes. Not the way it did last night when she was on top of me.

I want to see that smile again.

I hope I get the chance.

The voices inside of my head demand answers I just don't have to give.

Who are you running from, Tali?

Would you have told me if I hadn't forced you away?

Could I have protected you from whatever is haunting you?

Can I still?

I want to...I want you...

Chapter Fourteen
CRISTIAN

"I came here because what happened last night was real. More real than anything I've ever felt before."

"Too real for your liking, though? So real you didn't know how to handle it?" Tali pushes past me, and I let out a loud moan as she hits my shoulder.

Tali jumps, clapping a hand over her mouth. "Oh no, I'm so sorry! Are you okay?"

I grit my teeth and squeeze my eyes shut for the few seconds of excruciating pain to subside. "Yeah," I rasp.

Her hand grazes my arm, her fingertips dancing along my prickled skin. Christ, I want those fingertips in so many other places right now, preferably doing devious things to take my mind off of my agony. "Do you need anything?" she murmurs.

"I can think of a few ways you can make that up to me."

She raises her hand to give me a swat and stops herself mid-swing. Her eyes fall to my shoulder. "Consider yourself lucky."

"Thank you," I grunt. "I don't see you as the girl who shows mercy, but I appreciate it,"

"I don't know if you deserve it, though." She twists away from me, sauntering back into the apartment, her slim hips swinging with each step she takes. Good God, I want to feel those long, toned legs wrapped around my waist as I fuck her against this railing.

I may not know who I'm fighting against in this war, but I know who I'm *not*.

Every second that passes convinces me more and more that the people I'm looking for don't include the Severinovs.

That's why I'm here, because I can't think rationally where Tali is concerned.

Whatever this woman has done to me — to my heart and to my head — has led me back to her, again and again.

I'm always driven by emotion — good, bad, or otherwise.

Not ideal for a mafia enforcer.

Nine times out of ten, it puts me in a very fucking precarious position.

Today, I'm hoping for a different position.

Many different positions, as a matter of fact.

And they may be dangerous, too, in their own way.

Just not the life-threatening kind.

I reach out and grab Tali's arm.

She doesn't resist.

She doesn't try to flip me over her head.

I take both as positive signs.

"What do you want, Cristian? Because I really don't have much more to give."

"There are people looking to kill me and my family."

"Join the club," she scoffs. "This is our life. Did you miss the memo?"

"Whoever is after me killed my dad back in Sicily and one of his associates here a couple of weeks ago. These people want to destroy my family. They want to take over our shipping business and our coastal territories because the empire my father built is worth billions. Everyone wants a piece of it, groups from all over the world are conspiring against my family right now. They've gotten close to me, Tali. Right here in Monaco." I let out a deep sigh. "My uncle worked for one of those groups. He tried to have me killed the other night. But things went sideways, and he got sniped by one of his own goons instead. It was actually that guy who bit off my ear, not a seagull."

Tali is quiet for a second before her lips lift into a tiny smile. "I thought your bird watching story was a little weak."

"The bottom line is, I don't know who I'm even fighting right now. My family needs me. They're at risk, too. I have a lot to protect right now, and a lot of enemies who don't want us to win. It's not fair to drag you into that. So when I said last night that the timing wasn't right, it wasn't a bullshit excuse." I raise my hand to her cheek, not sure if she's going to try to break one or all of my fingers, but hey, it's worth the risk to just touch her. I'm already operating with a bum shoulder. I can do without a finger or two. "I didn't mean to hurt you."

"Okay," she says after a few minutes, twisting her long ponytail around a finger. "I'm sorry about your dad. I really am. But did you really feel the need to come here and tell me all of that so I'd forgive you? When there are so many nameless and faceless people hunting you down?" She rolls her eyes. "You didn't need to bother. I'm a big girl. But, fine. You're forgiven. Now get the hell out so I can go for my run."

"No," I say, catching her ponytail between my fingers and gently fisting it to tug her back toward me. "I don't want your forgiveness."

She gasps as I flip her around and back her against the glass door. "Oh yeah?" she hisses. "So what do you want, then? Because I'm not the type to give second chances, Marcone."

I lean into her, breathing in the scent of spearmint and strawberries. "I kind of figured. But I'm hoping you'll make an exception. Just this one time."

"I know what happens when you trust too soon and too freely," she whispers. "I've seen what it can do to people. To their lives. I don't want to be a victim again."

My brow furrows. "I can't ever see you as a victim. I know who you are. You'd never let yourself get caught in that kind of a trap."

"You don't know me. You don't know anything about me or what I'm dealing with."

"But I do," I whisper, letting her dark hair cascade down her back. I snake my good arm around her waist. "You've shown me who you really are again and again. I know you're having a rough time dealing with everything you've lost. And I also know you won't rest until you have achieved everything you want for your future. Don't doubt yourself. It's not who you are."

"I told you before. Sometimes you just don't have any options. You have to deal with what you've been dealt…what you've allowed yourself to be dealt."

"I don't believe that," I say as her eyes drop to the floor. "I've seen you fight for what you want. I've seen you render people sterile when you *don't* get what you want."

She giggles softly and the sound makes my cock twitch. "I know who you are, deep down, and that woman doesn't let anything stand in her way. She's strong, smart, and she believes in herself. She's..." I swallow hard as her eyes meet mine once again. "She's fucking amazing."

"Cristian..." My name tumbles from her lips just before I crush my mouth against hers, finally getting the taste I've fantasized about for far too long. I back her into the apartment, my hand wrapped around her back, fingertips digging into her spine as she bucks against me. Her head drops back, exposing the smooth column of her neck, and I drag my tongue over her soft, sweet-smelling skin.

A tiny moan escapes her mouth as I nip at her ear, tugging it gently with my teeth. She presses her hands into my hips, pushing me into her. My cock thickens against the slick fabric of her running tights and she gasps as I thrust against her.

I tug at the ponytail holder in her hair and slide it out, letting her glossy dark hair fall over her shoulders. She shakes it back, her arms sliding up my torso until her eyes fly open and she suddenly jumps back. "Oh my God! What about your arm? I don't want to hurt you."

I shake my head. "I don't care about my arm. I just want you, the way I wanted you last night. The way I wanted you when I first saw you on the beach when you threatened to have me arrested for trespassing."

She lets out a breathless giggle. "Well, you know, I *am* a ruthless one."

I nod. "I know. And I fucking love that about you."

"I still think you're a cocky and sarcastic asshole."

"And you just kissed me, so what does that say about you?"

"That maybe I'm not as smart as you say I am."

"Or maybe you're smarter." I wink, tugging the hem of her tank top.

"If I was so smart, I'd make you leave," she whispers.

"You also know I'd never go." I slide the top up over her head and toss it to the floor, dragging my fingers over the tops of her heaving breasts, smashed together in a tight sports bra. "That looks uncomfortable. I think we need to get it off. Right now." I reach around her back, gritting my teeth as my fingers work the tiny clasps on the bra strap. Goddammit! I never use two hands. Ever.

But this bra is fighting me hard. And I only have one hand to dedicate to this mission.

"You're having some trouble."

"I can get it."

I try a few more times, silently willing the clasp to please show me some mercy.

It doesn't.

I roll my eyes. This getting shot thing is really killing my mojo. And I'm in serious danger of losing my man card right now.

Tali reaches behind her back and undoes the clasp, pulling the bra over her head and letting it fall to the floor next to her. She laces her fingers with mine, backing into a bedroom off the hallway. Her perfect tits bounce as she moves, and my mouth waters in anticipation of devouring her.

Every last drop.

She drops my hands, her own going to work on my shirt. She takes her time, sliding my shirt off the bad shoulder, exposing the taped-up wound. Her fingers graze the area. "Does it hurt?"

"Only when you touch it."

She gasps, her hand flying off of the wound. "I'm sorry!"

I snicker and she bats my other arm. "You really are an ass."

"Yeah, and you love that about me. Just admit it."

She works my belt and my jeans, forcing them to the floor. I step out of them, kicking them off of my feet. "It adds to your charm." Her soft hand dips into my boxer briefs, grasping my hard cock. "So does this."

I let out a low groan. "Fuck, you're good at that."

"I'm good at a lot of other things, too. Wanna see?" She flashes a seductive smirk, and I want to bite it off those devious lips.

Fuck, yeah, I do!

She drags her hands down the front of my chest, tracing over the inked lines and swirls that cover my skin. Her lips follow, navigating a very determined path, one that has me harder than an iron rod. She pushes my boxers down, my cock springing to life without the constraint of fabric. Falling to her knees, she takes me into her mouth, so deep, the head of my dick hits the back of her throat.

I fist her hair as she licks and nips and tugs and sucks.

Christ, if sucking cock was an Olympic sport, my girl Tali would take the gold every single time.

She squeezes my balls, kneading them as her mouth works tirelessly, massaging every inch of my cock with her tongue. Her lips are pursed, her hot wet mouth so tight...

Oh, Christ.

I can't think about her tight wet anything right now or else I'll lose my shit.

I'm already operating with a handicap.

I can't blow my load early, too.

Not until I'm deep inside of that tight, wet pus—

Fuuuck.

Her tongue is working the length of my dick hard and fast, nipping at my slit. My knees buckle, my one hand tangled in her hair.

"Get up here," I growl, gently tugging her head back. Her eyes are hooded, the normally bright blue eyes now dark with the same lust coursing through me. With one final lick, she slides up the length of my body, careful to avoid my dead arm. "What's the matter? You didn't like that?"

"I fucking loved it. I just want to see what other tricks you've got," I whisper against her mouth, my tongue dipping into her lips. I rub my hand over her ass, looping my fingers into the waistband of the leggings. "We need to get these off. Now."

"What, are you in some kind of rush? Aren't there people out there who want you dead? Isn't it safer in here with me?"

"I don't know. You're dangerous, Tali. Very fucking dangerous for me," I mutter against her lips before plunging back into her eager mouth. Our tongues tangle and twist, coiling heat flowing between us. She backs away, pushing her leggings down while gazing at me through thick, dark eyelashes.

"No," I rasp. "That's my job."

"But you only have one arm."

"I only have one dick and one tongue, too. Trust me, I don't disappoint."

She smirks and lets out a squeal as I flip her around so the back of her legs are against the bed. I lift her with my one good side and lie her back on the bed, slowly rolling the leggings down the length of her legs. I pull them off, flinging them backward as I drop to my knees in front of her. Her legs fall open, her sweet pussy beckoning me, begging me to taste. I dip my head between her thighs, jutting out my tongue and delving into her. I stroke her clit with my thumb, pressing it gently at first, then flicking it faster as my tongue plunges deeper.

She gasps, clutching the bedsheet, her back arching as I fuck her with my mouth. "Oh my God!" she screams, thrusting hard against me. I work my fingers deep inside of her, keeping my thumb in place as she writhes on the bed, her wails shattering the silence.

And what an incredible sound it is.

I could listen to it forever.

And if there are people on the beach below her penthouse, they're listening to it, too.

I don't need my other hand as long as I have this magical tongue.

Good thing nobody tried to slice that shit off.

That would be a much worse handicap.

Her legs lock closed around my head, keeping me in place.

As if I'd ever want to leave.

Her juices flow into my greedy mouth, and I drink in every drop. But it's not enough.

It won't ever be enough.

Her body quivers and quakes on the mattress as the orgasm tears through her, and I know for sure that my inability to get her damn bra off is long forgotten.

Fucking redemption.

Now for my next trick...

I pull her up and...fuck. I need to stare. Just for a second.

Her hair is tousled, cheeks flushed and glowing, her eyes glitter with desire. But that smile...the one I'd wanted so badly to see again...it's there.

Wide, bright, and happy.

Just like the one from last night.

I'm not the best when it comes to reading people. I'm the first to admit it.

I'm rash and impulsive. I act first, think never, and it's cost me a hell of a lot over the years.

I've made so many wrong moves and put myself in harm's way too many times to count.

This time is different.

And her face at this moment tells me exactly what I want to know.

What I need to know.

It *is* real, and she's all in.

Just like me.

I crawl onto the bed, straddling her, but she shakes her head. Still smiling, she slowly pushes me back onto the mattress and climbs on top of me. Her head dips over mine, but instead of grazing my mouth, her lips choose a different spot — the area covered by the bandage.

Right over my heart.

I could be dead right now.

This could actually be my version of heaven.

I run my hand down the slope of her back as she hovers over my cock. She gives it a few long strokes, rubbing the swollen head against her pussy.

It's so warm.

So wet.

I grip her hips, thrusting upward, plunging into her heat. I let out a low moan as her pussy swallows me whole. Her walls tighten around me, her muscles clenching me tight. She hovers over me, her hair falling forward and tickling my bare skin. Her eyes drift closed as her head tilts back. My thrusts get deeper as she rocks faster against me, her tits pressed against my chest. I take them into my mouth, one at a time, my tongue and teeth working each deep pink bud. Her pussy clenches as I taunt her with my mouth, her slick walls tightening more and more with each passing second.

With every ounce of strength I have, I roll her over so that she's on her back, staring up at me. I drive my hips forward, plunging deeper into her slick heat. Her body trembles below me, her fingernails lancing my back so violently, it makes me cringe.

Her mewls have turned into full-fledged cries for God, her body convulsing against mine. I drive into her, her pussy coaxing me deeper and deeper until I don't know where I end and where she begins. She pulls me down to her, her teeth tugging at my lips, coaxing them open. Our frenzied bodies slide against each other, our skin prickled with beads of sweat. She locks her legs around my waist, urging me closer until the head of my dick hits the spot that makes her scream so loud, for a second, I'm afraid the windows will shatter.

A tingling sensation in my gut ignites, the erotic explosion blasting through every limb as I drown in her juices. My mind is blank, my body deliciously numb as my cock throbs and pulsates deep in her pussy. I thrust into her one more time, letting out a low growl as my own orgasm ravages me. I squeeze my eyes shut. My toes curl as I collapse onto my hands, losing myself inside of her.

Forgetting in that second that I'm not wearing a condom.

I guess I'm just so preoccupied with dodging contract killers that I forgot to stick one in my pocket before taking my life in my hands and walking over here.

I take a deep breath, not that it does a damn thing to calm my heart which is beating out of control, thumping against my chest like a hammer to a nail.

Jesus, this pussy is the equivalent of sexual heroin.

One taste, and I'm a fucking addict for life.

I definitely need to stay alive now.

"Wow," Tali whispers, flinging a hand over her eyes. "And you weren't even a hundred percent."

"Listen," I say, plucking her hand off of her face. "I am *always* running at a hundred percent down there. Let's just get that straight right now."

She giggles. "That's so Italian of you."

"Fucking right. That's one of the best things about us."

"What am I doing with you?"

"Right now, you're admiring my sexual prowess, and while I don't want this part to end too quickly, I'd really like to be doing other things."

"Other X-rated things, I hope?"

I nod, running my fingers down the sides of her bright pink cheeks. She has that *just got fucked* look and she's never been more beautiful to me than she is right now. "Yeah. Except…we, uh, didn't use anything." I lift an eyebrow. "Should I be worried?"

"About your life, yes." She smirks. "But not about a bambino. I'm on the pill, so you're clear."

"Great. So it wasn't a ploy to take over half my family's assets, then."

"No," she says in a mock teasing tone, tapping a finger against her chin. "I didn't even think of that. Maybe if you hadn't been such a cocky asshole for so long, I might have concocted that plan on my own."

"I told you. It's all part of my charm."

"Yes, but nobody wants to be charmed by a snake."

"Worked for you. I knew I'd eventually break you down." I flip onto my back and let out a sigh. "And now look at you. You're dying for it now. You can't get enough. I can tell you're fighting yourself not to mount me again right now."

"You are really unbelievable." With a chuckle, she kicks a leg over me, sliding herself closer.

"I told you I wouldn't disappoint."

"I had complete faith in your abilities." With one swift motion, she jumps on top of me, tucking her hair behind her ears. "You have a lot of very special...*gifts*."

With a smirk, I grab her hips, massaging them. "Oh yeah, I do. And they keep on giving, too."

She clutches her heart. "How did I ever get so lucky?"

I laugh, and she joins in. This is the oddest, post-coital exchange I think I've ever had. I've never spent any bit of time looking at women I've slept with afterward. I don't notice things like their skin tone or the glimmer in their eyes after I've launched them into orbit with my massive cock.

Yes, it is massive.

And yes, it can rocket, a fact I've just proven yet again with Tali.

I haven't ever cared enough to take that long hard look.

But I do now.

Unfortunately, I don't have time to sit here and stare.

Because while I let my dick lead me here, I haven't come away with anything useful to my family.

I had a job to do.

And it didn't get done.

That means we're still no closer to the truth about what happened to Dad and Daniel.

Alek told me where to find Tali.

I need him to give me a little bit more than that.

"What do you say? Can you handle another round?" Tali whispers, tracing a finger over my chest. "Or was that last one too much for you?"

I hold her tight, not wanting to let her go, not wanting to face the demons who are no doubt lurking, waiting for me to appear.

I'd much rather stay here with my dick buried inside of Tali.

But I have to think about my family.

Their lives.

And I know I can't stay.

"It could never be enough," I murmur, giving her ass a squeeze. "But I have to go."

A look of concern eclipses the brightness of her seductive smile, and she bites down on her lower lip. "Cristian, what happens when you leave here?"

"Well, if *I'm* lucky, I get back to my place without getting sniped."

She rolls her eyes. "I'm serious. Why don't you let me—?"

"No," I say without letting her finish. "No way. If we'd have stayed together last night, you could have gotten hurt. Or worse. I'm not doing that to you. I won't put you in danger."

"I handle myself pretty well, you know." She flexes her arms. "And I have use of *all* limbs, just saying. I can do some serious damage."

"You're pretty badass, I'll give you that. But no, I have to find answers and I need to do it alone."

"Okay," she says in a soft voice.

"Hey, don't look so disappointed. I'll be back for a repeat performance."

"Promise?"

"You better fucking believe it," I growl, pulling her close. Our mouths crash against each other—hot, hungry, and intense. I fist her hair, devouring her with a desire that cannot be quelled.

Yeah, I need to stay the fuck out of harm's way.

I need this woman in my life.

When our lips part, I lean my forehead against hers. "Go for your run, but don't get too tired out. I'll take care of that later."

She smiles. "Deal."

I manage to get dressed using my one working arm and it surprisingly doesn't take me ten years.

Small steps.

"Be careful," she whispers, running her hand down the front of my shirt.

I graze her lips with mine. "I will." I reach between her legs, my fingers sliding against her pussy. "This is reason enough for me to stay alive."

She grins. "Are you sure you have to go?"

"Yeah," I say in a gruff voice. "But I'll be back." I grab my phone from the table where I left it and glance at the screen. About a million texts from Diego and Jak.

They won't be thrilled to find out what I've been doing for the past hour, that's for sure.

Neither will Tali's dickhead brother Kaz.

I make a mental note to tell him about it next time I see him. Really get his ass in a twist.

And if he tries to kill me...well, he'll be in good company.

"Do you want me to get you a car? I can call Sasha, my head of security. He will arrange it."

I shake my head. "Thanks, but I can handle it. I'm not hiding, Tali." A teasing smirk lifts my lips. "Is it cool that I call you that? Are we friends now?"

She smirks. "So it wasn't just sex, then?"

"No," I say, interlocking my fingers with hers. "It wasn't. Not to me."

"Oh," she whispers, her cheeks flushing a deep pink. "Well, in that case, yes. You can call me Tali."

I smack her ass and she lets out a playful shriek. "Trust me, we're gonna be really good friends, Tali."

"The best," she murmurs, kissing me one last time before I make it to the door.

I leave her apartment and ride the elevator back to the lobby, staring at the keyboard on my phone. What am I supposed to tell Diego when he asks where the hell I've been all morning?

Somehow I don't think he'd appreciate hearing about how I was *making friends* with the alleged enemy.

Chapter Fifteen
TALI

"I just don't like the guy," Kaz snarls as we rush through Cote d'Azur Airport in Nice, France with Leo and Myla on our heels. "He seems like a real dick."

It's hard for me to argue since I've had that same thought more times than I can count. "He's kind of an acquired taste."

Kaz looks at me, his blue eyes wide open in disgust. "Don't even think of saying another word about tasting anything, Tali!"

I giggle with a small huff, hoisting a duffel bag over my shoulder. "You can relax, okay? We're friends." Mm, yes, friends with many deliciously erotic benefits. But I leave out that part as we hustle through the terminal toward the security gates. "How come we can never be on time for anything, guys? Is it really in the DNA?"

"Seems so," my other brother Leo snickers as we race past crowds of people milling about in the terminal. Doesn't look like anyone other than us has anywhere to go. It would be so nice if they'd just get the hell out of our way, though. "But this guy, Tali. You're sure he's okay?"

Oh, yes. Much more than okay. Tiny butterflies in my belly flutter their wings fast and furious, a vivid remembrance of the sheer bliss I experienced only hours earlier manifesting itself yet again. "He's safe, guys. Relax."

"I don't get it," Kaz grumbles. "For weeks I listened to you bitch about the asshole who owns the hotel next door, and now he shows up at your front door? Wanting more than a simple truce, I'm sure. And even though I'm glad you finally decided to kick that French fuck to the curb, I don't like the replacement." Sparks fly from his eyes as he digs around in his bag for his passport.

"Don't worry about him," Leo's girlfriend Myla whispers to me. "You know he's just worried about leaving you here by yourself."

"Yeah, but I'm not by myself. I have Alek," I say a little bit too loudly.

Kaz scoffs. "Please. Like he's going to be of any help. He's too focused on his own shit to worry about yours."

"That's not fair, Kaz. He has a lot on his plate right now." I poke Kaz in the side. "Be a little more sensitive. You only have to run security for a casino. He has to run everything else."

Kaz rolls his eyes. "He gets to keep a shit ton more, too. I'd run more if I had my hand deeper into the pot."

"Yeah, but with you running more, there might not be a pot to dip our hands into," Leo quips.

I snicker because he has a good point. Kaz is kind of a loose cannon, and it's true that the entire livelihood of our family would be resting in very unstable hands if it was left up to him. Alek has his issues, yes. But he's been able to take control of our family's businesses and resurrect them since Dad died. It's more than any one of us has been able to handle. Then again, none of us have that sadistic streak.

We each have our own skillset.

Kaz and I are the assassins.

Leo is the businessman.

And Alek? He's the catch-all. He is a master negotiator and has no fear about dealing with any of our rivals. My dad trained him to take over practically since birth, and he's picked up plenty of his own tricks along the way. Brutal, vicious, deadly tricks nobody ever taught him. But his priority is always the family, so he does whatever he needs to take care of his own. He watches everything, sizes up our threats, and directs from the sidelines. He knows who to tag in and when. And if they don't deliver? You can be sure he will. He's his own secret weapon. He doesn't dole out kill orders for his own targets if they don't cooperate with his wishes. He works them over in his own way, and if they resist, they're dead and stripped of their livelihoods.

Absolutely fucking ruthless.

If he's smiling at you, you never quite know if it's because you've done something right or something very wrong that he feels the need to correct.

If that happens, consider yourself screwed.

And dead.

I love that about him, that black and white view he has about pretty much everything, but I can see where it makes Kaz uneasy. Alek has unconventional ways of working that have put our family under fire in the past, and with me being on my own here, it's no wonder why Kaz is apprehensive.

But my twin brother should have a little more faith in me.

"I will be just fine." And then it dawns on me that ever since I've been floating on this post-coital high, I haven't thought about Alain, sending him packing with his threats, and what might very well become my reality if he decides to pull the proverbial trigger and give me up.

Suddenly, my feet go from floating above the clouds to slamming down on the hard concrete.

It's a harsh descent, to say the least.

If Kaz wants to really worry about something, it should be Alain Leclercq.

He alone can do way more damage than Cristian and Alek put together, and then multiply it by a thousand.

And that realization makes my heart sink into my Nikes.

But I force a smile, because what else can I do other than *nothing*?

"Everything is going to be just fine," I say, trying to convince myself of it even though I have zero faith that it will be the case. I have that little prick breathing down my neck with all of his threats, keeping me awake at night. How much longer am I going to allow myself to be his little puppet?

Part of me wants to run to Alek and tell him the whole, sordid story, but the other part is afraid that it will send Alek right into Alain's trap.

I can't let that happen. I still have time to figure this out. I won't let him destroy my family or our future.

I'll give myself up first so that doesn't happen.

So long as everyone else stays safe.

It's my fate that should hang in the balance, not theirs.

So, yes. Everything will be just fine.

For them, because I'll make it so.

I have to.

"It had better be," Kaz grunts as he steps into the security line. By some miracle, there aren't huge crowds clogging up the checkpoint.

"You need to stop worrying." I manage a smile. "And you need to hurry or else you're going to miss your flight!" I look over at Leo and Myla. "You, too. I know you have a little bit more time since you're going in two directions, but still. Get moving!" I give them kisses and hugs, watching Leo hustle Myla to the front of the line.

Kaz opens his arms, and I fling myself into them. "I'm going to miss you," I say in a tearful voice, knowing that for the foreseeable future if I want to see him, it'll have to be over FaceTime. "I'm going to miss you so much."

"I'm going to miss you, too," he replies in a gruff voice. "Tali, I'm serious. You need to be careful and watch your back. You have a good security team. Not great by any fucking stretch, but decent. You need more guys."

I laugh, tears gathering in the corners of my eyes. "You're just saying that because you think you're the best head of security on the planet."

"There's no thinking involved, kid. It's a fact. Don't ever forget it. And if you need me, I'm only a flight away, understand?"

I nod, sniffling. "Gotcha."

He ruffles my hair and gives me one last bear hug before sneaking into the growing line. "Don't forget," he says.

"I won't," I reply, watching them all disappear into the throngs of frenzied passengers trying to make their flights. It's been a hard year, and having them all here for a while made the anniversary of Dad's death easier to handle.

But now they're all gone. My support system has officially dispersed, and it's time for me to rely on myself again to figure out how the hell to navigate the shark-infested political waters of Monaco and my future here.

If there's a future.

I turn to head back through the terminal, the deep ache weighing me down like there's a cement block lodged in my chest.

Now that I have my sights set on what my life can become, I need to put these demons to rest for good.

The big question is the one that's been haunting me for weeks.

How?

Chapter Sixteen
CRISTIAN

I don't bother to go back to my hotel right away. I can't, not without any information other than the noises Tali makes when an orgasm rips through her. That's not going to be useful to Diego or Jak.

But it's plenty useful for me.

She can't have been acting. It had to have been real, every carnal second of it.

But I'll talk to Alek because I know he'll confirm that Diego's suspicions are wrong.

And if someone happens to jump out of a bush with a machete along the way, I'll remember to question before I attack back.

I keep my eyes moving in all directions as I walk to meet Alek at a street café, never missing a beat. The street is filled with people — heading to and from the beach, visiting the shops and cafés that line the narrow road, and bike riding in the late morning sunshine.

Everyone seems happy and relaxed.

I bet nobody is trying to kill any of them.

I wiggle the fingers of my dead arm just to keep the blood flowing as a distant memory assaults my mind. I haven't thought about it in so long, maybe because it reminds me of what can happen when you lose your edge and when you succumb to emotion.

Which is exactly what happened to my father.

The thought chills me now, even as the scorching hot sun blasts my skin with its rays.

Maybe there is another reason why I've kept the memory buried.

Maybe I don't want to acknowledge that I've fallen into the same trap over and over again, something he berated me for until the day he died at the hand of our faceless enemies.

God, I haven't thought about her in years...

It was my sister Gianna's ninth birthday, and she'd wanted a unicorn cake. Of course, in a house otherwise full of males, nobody knew how the hell to fulfill that wish, but Dad worked tirelessly to try to make one for her. With zero artistic talent and no knowledge of baking or cake decorating, it fell a little short.

Okay, a lot short.

One person saved the day, and almost stole it in practically the same breath.

Dad's girlfriend, Maria. She was young, beautiful, and me and my brothers all had hard-ons for her. We were a bunch of horny boys, and she was always parading around in short, low-cut dresses. It was tough not to stare, tougher to not fantasize.

She won us over pretty quickly, and for the first time since Mom died, Dad seemed happy and relaxed. We didn't know much about his job at that point because we were still young, but we knew it was stressful.

It kept him up late at night and the people he worked with made visits twenty-four-seven. We always tried to overhear bits of conversation, but they were always careful not to say anything that wasn't behind tightly closed doors.

Whenever we asked about his job, he would just say he was in the fishing business.

Made sense, since we ate a lot of it.

We'd always try to get him out of his office, to watch television with us, to play board games, or to take us out to the yard to throw around a baseball.

But he was always all about his job, and he told us how important it was to be dedicated to your work, how if you take too many breaks, you could be replaced. And if you're replaced, you could lose everything.

And then Maria came along and everything changed. All of a sudden, he chose to not let his work bury him. He chose life instead, life with his kids, life with his beautiful girlfriend. It actually felt like we were part of a family instead of being a bunch of kids who were on the outside looking in, wondering what it might feel like to be part of one.

I guess Dad liked the glimpse he got, too.

He still worked, but he was around more. So was Maria.

We felt like a family.

So naturally, when Gianna wanted this cake, everyone pitched in. Together.

But it did end up taking a woman's touch to get it just perfect. And Maria's rescued cake didn't disappoint. Gianna was over the moon about it, and Dad couldn't have been happier that his little princess got exactly what she wanted.

Unfortunately, she also got something she hadn't asked for, something that haunted my father until the very end of his life.

Something none of us will ever forget, although we never talk about it.

Ever.

It broke us, nearly beyond repair.

And became the big ass elephant in the room that followed us everywhere, no matter where we went.

It was always there, always weighing on us, but silent, so that we never had to relive the horror.

Right before we were all about to enjoy Gianna's birthday cake, Maria had taken her upstairs to get her ready for her little party. She was promised a birthday look of bows and glitter and rainbows, but in the end, that wasn't what Maria delivered.

Not by a long shot.

And suddenly the memory is alive in my mind, as vivid and real as if it had just happened yesterday...

I walk up the stairs to Gianna's bedroom, my feet creaking on the hardwood floor. "G!" I call out.

But there is no answer. From either of them.

It's completely silent. No laughter, no singing, no excited chatter.

I push open the door to Gianna's bedroom, and an icy cold sensation snakes through me, my body clearly preparing for something my mind can't wrap itself around.

My eyes take in the scene, my feet rooted to the floor. I want to run. I want to scream. But I can't. I'm frozen. Paralyzed. Consumed with a fear

I've never in my life known.

Maria rises from her spot on the floor next to Gianna's, holding a cake cutting knife dripping with blood.

My baby sister's blood.

Maria's eyes are wild, her once-beautiful face twisted into a mask of pure evil, her eyes narrowed to slits.

My heart thumps hard against my chest. I open my mouth to scream, but no words come out.

"Cristian!" My dad bellows from the dining room. "Let's get this fashion show started! We're all waiting!"

Maria smiles, but it's not the sweet smile I've gotten used to seeing over the past months. It's sinister. Malicious. And vengeful. "Yell, Cristian. Scream for your father so he can see how it feels to lose someone he loves and not be able to do a thing to stop it." She steps forward. "You want to hurt me. I can tell. But I know you won't because you're a good boy and good boys don't hurt women. Especially pretty women, right?"

But I don't answer her. I don't yell. I don't make a single sound.

I just do what I always do.

I leap at Maria, forgetting that she's a woman. Because she's not. She's a beast. A devil. And I claw the knife out of her hands, biting, pinching, and kicking with everything in me. I tear hair out of her scalp, slamming her against a wall, and close my hand around her throat. She squirms and gasps for air, kicking her legs around, fighting me off with every ounce of strength she has left.

Crack!

Suddenly, she stops moving. Blood drizzles out of the wound in the center of her forehead and I let go of her, watching her crash to the ground. The sound of the metal gun clattering to the floor behind me is followed by my father's screams.

When I turn away from Maria's limp body, I see my father crumbled onto the floor next to Gianna, surrounded by my other brothers. I'll never forget hearing him weep, praying for God's mercy and forgiveness, begging for her life, apologizing for his misdeeds.

It was the first time in my life that I felt helpless...hopeless...and broken.

I remember thinking at that very moment that our family had been shattered, and I didn't know if it could ever be pieced back together.

I pick up the pace as if I'm trying to shake the memory and leave it behind me, where I've tried to keep it buried ever since that night.

I know it's never far from Diego's mind since he never misses an opportunity to remind me that I don't think before I unleash my vengeance.

It turns out there was a lot we didn't know about Maria, and a lot more we never knew because I made sure she would never hurt anyone else in the family.

Me and my father.

Evidently, the whole *attack first, think never* thing is genetic.

It's in my blood.

It was in Dad's blood, too.

We found out that's why Maria hitched her wagon to Dad's in the first place. And that's when we learned what it was my father really did for a living. At Dad's order years earlier, Maria's family had been killed. They weren't the primary targets, but they were in the wrong place at the wrong time. And the hit was the result of pure rage, revenge he launched against a rival. Dad never considered the consequences, never thought there would ever be backlash for his directive.

How many times had I told myself the same thing before making some of my own stupid choices?

Years later, Maria showed up on the scene.

And he never saw it coming.

Never saw it coming.

I think he liked being normal and happy and a little less angry all of the time.

But he got sloppy. He trusted too much and opened himself and his family up to a horror beyond any of our worst nightmares.

That was the last time Dad let anyone in.

He didn't take unnecessary risks after that night.

But eventually, all of our mistakes come back to haunt us at one time or another.

By the grace of God, Gianna survived the attack. She was always so strong, so determined, and persistent as hell. No way was she going to lose that battle, even at such a young age.

It was a treacherous experience, one I pray I never have to live through again.

But something about that night always stuck with me, something that sits on the back burner, irking and taunting me.

His words...a chilling message that is forever branded into my memory.

Things aren't always what they seem, Cristian.

I try to shrug off the feeling of unease, but it's still there, knotting my gut.

Why? What the hell is he trying to tell me?

What the hell am I missing?

Where am I not looking?

And why the hell hasn't Jak come up with any leads yet?

I pull open the door to Café Bleu, stepping inside. It's not too crowded and I spot Alek sitting in the back of the place, calmly sipping from an espresso cup. I'm not sure why he wanted to meet here, but I didn't question it when he gave the address.

He may have information I need, so I decide to play nice.

At least, to start.

I weave through patrons, tables, and chairs to get to the far-off table nestled against a big picture window. He looks at me with his ice blue eyes and nods to one of the empty chairs. I pull one out and sit.

He takes another sip of his drink and sets the cup in the saucer. "You're in bad shape, Marcone."

I nod. "Yeah, it hasn't been an easy couple of days."

"What are you doing with my sister?"

"Do you want all of the sordid details, or just the CliffsNotes version?"

He leans forward, his fingers gripping the table. "I want to know why you're trying to put her in the line of fire."

I hold up my hands. "Whoa. I'm not putting her anywhere."

"She was with you the night you got shot, wasn't she?"

"Yeah."

"And what about the night your ear was bitten off? You almost landed on her when you escaped that chalet."

"How'd you know about that?"

He narrows his eyes. "I don't think you know who or what you're dealing with. My father had a lot of enemies, enemies I'm still warding off. Enemies my sister knows nothing about. I've kept a lot of things from her to keep her safe, and because she's not emotionally equipped to handle them yet. She's still grieving, and she needs time to process everything that's happened. And then all of a sudden, you show up on the scene and shit starts going sideways, all starting with that bomb."

"Wait, you think that was *me*?"

"I think there's a good chance you might know who did it, yeah." His mouth twists into a grimace.

"That's crazy."

"Is it?"

"Yes! I'm looking for my own answers, okay? The people who did this to me? They want me dead. My whole family, as a matter of fact. And they're getting closer. I came to you because I need to know who they are."

He lifts an eyebrow. "And you think I can help you? You think I *would* help you?"

"I think you know a lot more than you're letting on." My voice drops.

"I will protect my family with everything I have in me," he hisses.

I let out a dry laugh. "That's a bunch of bullshit. This morning, you told me where I could find Tali. Why did your tune change all of a sudden?"

"I needed to make sure you weren't trying to sink your claws into her to get to our businesses. After the bomb and you showing up afterward, I wasn't so sure." He takes another sip of espresso and looks at me. "Did you really think I was going to let you walk in there and not have an eye on you the entire time? I had guys outside of that door, just begging for a chance to take it off its hinges and fuck your shit up if you made one false move."

"That's pretty fucking disturbing, man. Just saying. I mean, it's your *sister*."

"I needed to make sure you were clear."

"And now you see that I was."

"I saw much more than I wanted to see, thank you very much. But, I'm still not convinced."

"You want me to go and fuck her again so you can get another look?" I hold up my phone. "I'll give her a call right now. I'm sure she'd be up to it. She seemed to have had a pretty good time with me before." I smirk. "Oh, but you already knew that, you perverted fuck."

Alek grits his teeth. "I can't have my family be associated with yours. I know why you're here in Monaco. I know your hotel is a bullshit front. I know who you're looking for, and I know why. You aren't the only one with eyes and ears everywhere. But make no mistake. We're not allies. Not even close. See, Daniel Tava agreed to sell his part of the shipping business to *me* just before he got killed. I bet you didn't know that, did you?" He shakes his head. "So now, the same bastards who are looking to take over your piece of the pie are looking to steal mine, too. He was killed just before word got out that he sold them to me. That hit-and-run looks bad for a lot of people, Marcone. Who was trying to keep Tava quiet? Who was trying to keep him from making any moves to sell? And when whoever killed him is found...and believe me, the fucknut will be found...they're going to be under fire, and so will everyone associated to them."

"Let me guess. You think I had something to do with that, too." I roll my eyes.

"Truth be told…" He pauses, his eyes narrowed. "No. But it doesn't matter what I think. It only matters what shit looks like to the enemy. And if the enemy thinks you steamrolled Tava because you didn't like that he was making deals behind your family's back after your dad was killed, then they'll be coming after you. And I don't need that hellfire raining down on me and my family if we're associated with you." His lips stretch into a thin line. "So now that I know you're not trying to make my family take the fall for this, and you're not on the hunt yourself to take us out, let me say something to you one last time. Stay the fuck away from Tali."

Chapter Seventeen
TALI

The wind whips through my hair as I accelerate around a turn headed back to the hotel strip after seeing my family off at the airport. I'm driving one of the hotel's cars, an Escalade that doesn't corner nearly as well as my own car does. Or rather, the way it *did*. But I don't want to think about my beloved Maserati right now and why it's permanently out of commission.

I'll have to face it all soon enough when I come clean to Alek.

The crashing waves of the Mediterranean bring me some semblance of comfort and peace. I haven't experienced either for as long as I can remember. A tiny fluttering sensation erupts in my belly, the memory of my body pressed against Cristian's earlier today still fresh in my mind.

God, what he did to me...

I can't explain it, can't rationalize it, can't really wrap my arms around it.

I hated the guy — while secretly lusting after him — only days earlier.

And now?

All of the barriers I'd slapped up to protect my heart from any further devastation have been stripped away, one by one.

He broke me down just like he joked that he would.

And I let him. I gave him so much of myself, so much more than just my body. I let him into my fragile heart. I gave him access to my deepest thoughts and feelings, and in return, he gave me hope.

Something I thought was long gone.

The delicious swirly feeling is fast replaced by a heaviness that reminds me of a loose end I need to tie up.

The destructive secret that can quickly terminate my plans and dreams for the future.

With Cristian.

With my family.

A lot of things hang in the balance right now, and it's going to take a hell of a lot more than prayers to tip the scales in my direction.

I need someone merciless, someone calculating, and someone with a sick and twisted sense of justice to help me out of this.

My brother Alek. He can help me. He always knows exactly what to do and how to handle bad situations.

Translation: He's all calm and controlled on the surface, but underneath the icy and stoic exterior there lies a fucking monster aching to be unleashed. He doesn't come out to play often, but when he does, heads roll.

Literally.

That's why he's the boss.

My phone buzzes on the passenger's seat, and I grab it.

Speaking of the devil himself...

I switch it over to the car speaker and click Accept. "Hey, what's up?"

"Where are you right now?" Alek's voice sounds a little off. Not that it's cause for concern. He always sounds a little off. But this time there's an edge to it, one that tells me he's not his normal, chipper self.

"I'm headed back to the hotel. I just dropped the guys and Myla off at the airport. Why?"

He lets out a frustrated sigh. "I'm going into a meeting right now. But I'll be done in about an hour. I need you to come by my office."

"Why am I always coming to you?" I say in a teasing tone. "Why don't you ever slum it and come down to me?"

"I'm serious, Tali. This is important."

"Hmm. Okay, then. Sounds like we're going to need cocktails."

"You have no idea. I'll see you in about an hour." *Click.*

Alek isn't an alarmist. If he says something is important, to everyone else on Earth it roughly translates to a life-or-death situation.

I shuffle through some scenarios in my mind, pretty damn certain that whatever it is can't be as bad as what I'm going to hit him with when I get to his office. If he's pissed off now, when I'm done with him, he's going to go ballistic.

But I'm not going to think about that right now. No, there is something...someone...else demanding the top spot in my devilish little mind. And there's no time like the present to start sharing my inner-most desires with him.

I accelerate as Cristian's hotel comes into view. There are only a couple of high-end cars parked out front, and there's no valet in sight. I furrow my brow. Where are all of the guests? Nobody is checking in or out?

I take a gamble that I won't get towed, park the Escalade, and hurry through the main entrance.

With a quick look around, I notice that I'm the only person in the lobby.

That's weird.

It's one of the busiest seasons of the year. How does this hotel not have any people roaming around? I don't care how exclusive Cristian claims it to be. And there's no way his guests are all at the beach right now.

The click of shoes on the shiny marble lobby floor makes me jump, and I twist around with a gasp to find Cristian behind me. "Oh my God! You scared the hell out of me!"

Cristian looks at me. He doesn't smile, doesn't wink, doesn't speak. He makes no moves to hug me or kiss me.

He just stares.

"So where are all of your guests? This place looks completely empty," I say with a smile, waving a hand around me.

"I told you, it's very exclusive. My guests are big on privacy, and our villas cater to their every need."

"But the parking lot is empty. How do they come and go?" I furrow my brow. "I still don't understand—"

"Is that why you came here, Tali?" he interrupts in a harsh tone, his eyes guarded and cold. "To investigate me and the way I run my hotel?"

I let out a tiny gasp, an uneasy feeling slithering through my insides. I wipe the palms of my hands on my skirt and lick my lips. My heart thunders in my chest as the realization smacks me in the face.

I'd come here because I saw what my life could actually become...because of the hope he'd given me.

Was it all bullshit?

Because the look on his face tells me he'd much rather see an army of cockroaches scattering over the marble floor tiles instead of me.

Goddammit! I put so much trust in him so soon! Why haven't I learned my freaking lesson? What in the hell is it going to take for me to finally see things clearly?

The old Tali would never have let him inside.

The old Tali would have seen through to the core of his black heart.

I swallow hard. For Christ's sake! Grab back some of the control you just threw at him, dammit! "No. I, uh, I was hoping to talk to you."

He rubs the back of his neck, looking in every direction but mine. "You should have called."

"Well, I might have," I snap. "If you'd have given me your number. But I guess that's part of your little game, right? Best way to make a clean break?"

"Look, it's not a game. It's just not going to happen. I'm sorry if I gave you a different impression before, but this thing...we can't do it again. It shouldn't have happened in the first place." He turns to walk over to the vacant front desk, leaving me fuming in the center of the empty lobby.

My mouth drops open. Holy shit, did I just hear those words drip from his beautiful, bitable lips? And damn me for even thinking anything about those lips other than me splitting them with my bare hands! I feel the steam billowing out of my ears now. I run past him, and shove myself in his path, getting in his face so he has no choice but to look at me. "You got what you wanted from me. You chased me down after I rejected you and fucked me harder than I ever thought possible." I shake my head. "God, I'm a complete idiot for believing anything that comes out of your sleazy, slimy mouth! This was all about the chase. You never gave a shit about anything but getting me into bed. And when you got that, you were done with me. You're a scumbag, and I hope your dick shrivels up and falls off!" My nostrils flare and I twist away from him, ready to stalk out of the lobby.

But, no.

Fuck no!

There's more to this story. Much more.

I haven't written the ending yet, but I'm sure as hell going to take a crack at it now.

Literally.

I turn back one more time, stomp over to him before he reaches the desk and clock him right in the jaw. I flex my fingers. Goddamn, that hurt!

But Cristian barely moves. His chest heaves, his eyes glowering at me like he wants to tear me in two.

And maybe he does. Maybe he should try.

I'll fuck his shit up! I'll mangle the rest of him that's still in one piece!

"You should go," he hisses.

"I hate you! I hated you from the second I heard your fucking asshole voice!" I scream, not giving a shit if any of his guests — wherever they are — hear the crazy bitch in the lobby. My voice echoes in the expansive space. I shove my hands at his chest. "I knew I couldn't trust you! I knew you were a lying snake who takes what he wants from people and then crushes them! You should take your olive-oil-eating ass back to Ginzoville, Italy! You bastard!" I raise my hand one more time for good measure, hoping to land another hit that'll send him crashing to his knees.

This time he's prepared.

He grabs my wrist, twisting my arm around my back, his deep gravelly voice gruff against my ear. And dammit, it still sends shivers down my spine even though I know he's a scumbag. "Are you gonna try that again?"

"You don't think I can handle it?" I seethe. "Do you have a death wish, asshole? Because that was me going easy on you! And I'm ready to play!"

He tightens his grip on my arm, and I grit my teeth. "I only have one arm, and yet I've managed to get you into a pretty compromising position. How do you expect to get out of it?"

I twist and turn and struggle, but he only holds me tighter. I narrow my eyes at him. "Let go of me or I'll bite off your other goddamn ear!"

"Why did you come here?" he growls. "Why the fuck did you come?"

I blink fast, my lips refusing to make the words that my brain is screaming right now. Oh my God, I want to take a fire poker and lance this bastard's face...just before I pop out his eyeballs! "Because I'm stupid!" I shriek, pounding against him to no avail. "I thought today meant something! I wanted to tell you what it meant to me, damn you! But you used me. You're just another womanizing asshole. I knew it," I hiss. "I *knew* it!"

"You don't know anything," he grunts, dragging me beyond the front desk. He pushes open a door and it slams shut behind us. Cristian's arm is still holding me in place, and a tiny part of me thinks he might just try to off me right here in this office.

Which is also empty.

Jesus Christ, doesn't he have any employees who actually *work*?

"Get your hands off of me," I say, my voice quivering with anger. And panic, if I'm being honest.

"You don't want me to take them off you," he says, the malice in his gaze morphing into fire. His eyes glow like little candles, the heat singeing me from the inside out. "You came because you want it even more now."

"Screw you," I breathe, the scent of his cologne making my brain fuzzier with each passing second. "You obviously don't realize what you had."

"Oh, but I do." He loosens his grip on me, his one hand reaching behind my head and fisting my hair. "I know exactly what I had. What I want again. And again. And again."

Our lips crush against each other, a mess of coiling tongues and unquenched desire. Before I even know what's happening, my blouse is torn open and my bra is around my ankles.

With one working hand. He's obviously honed his one-armed skills. That's just all sorts of impressive.

Our hands grope and grip and grab, working fast and furious to remove the rest of the fabric that's in the way of what our frenzied bodies crave so deeply. I manage to yank open Cristian's jeans and push them and his boxers to his knees. I grasp his thick cock and stroke it a few times until he lets out a low groan and flips me around so my back is to him. He shoves my skirt up over my hips, lining his cock up with my slit. He pushes me over a chair, grazing my opening with the head of his cock, gently at first as he kneads my breasts. His lips scorch a blissful path down the slope of my neck as he pushes himself into my heat, rubbing his length against my swollen clit with each jerk of his hips. With long, deep strokes he plunders me with such intensity, tears spring to my eyes. His hand is plastered across my chest, holding me tight against his own.

With pounding force, he thrusts deeper.

Harder.

Faster.

My body quivers and quakes, a blinding white light flashing across my eyes. Sparks ignite in my core, the explosion so swift and strong, my knees buckle. But Cristian doesn't let me go. His cock pulsates deep inside of me as he rubs my clit, the euphoria all-consuming. I clench my muscles, drawing him in farther, urging him to hit the spot that will cause my undoing right here, bent over this chair.

Oh God, he's so close…so close…

And that's when the party starts.

I squeeze my eyes shut, my screams for God piercing the otherwise still air.

I don't care who hears. I don't care if one of his employees comes barging in here.

They can watch.

And learn.

And be jealous as hell as this man launches me into the stratosphere!

Tremors rock my body as Cristian thrusts a few more times before we both collapse onto the chair, sweaty, breathless, and completely sated.

For now, at least.

I grip the back of the chair, my body humming with aftershocks that I hope stay with me for hours to come. I gulp in air, trying to settle my breathing before I ask the dreaded question...

What the hell just happened?

I peek over my shoulder, my chest still heaving as I drink in oxygen. "Care to explain?" I rasp.

He runs a hand through his hair, straightening up and stepping away from where I'm plastered over the chair. His eyes are hooded, his cock hanging between his legs, still half-hard and at the ready.

Oh, I can be ready, too...

I give my head a quick shake. No, stop! "You told me I should leave. That this can't happen. So what the hell message was your little stunt supposed to send?"

"I wanted you to go," he says.

"Fuck you!" I spit out the words, my heart aching with each syllable spoken.

"Tali, last night when I said it wasn't the right time...I meant it. I thought I could find a way. I really did. And everything I told you was the truth."

"Oh, yeah? And what about everything you didn't tell me?"

"I was honest with you last night and this morning."

"And what about just now? Am I your little fuck toy? You play with my head and then play with my pussy? Is that fun for you, Cristian?" I snarl, pulling my skirt back down over my hips.

"No," he murmurs. "It's fucking torture, Tali. This isn't what I wanted."

"Then why are you doing it, huh?" I sniffle, hating myself for being *that* pathetic head case of a girl.

"Because I have to. Because of the dangers out there."

"Oh, please! Give me a break!" I throw up my hands. "The dangers! You have to be kidding me! There are always targets on people like us, Cristian. Regardless of who we screw."

"You need to leave."

"Oh, don't worry. I'm getting the hell out of here. You'll never have to worry about me ever setting foot into your gaudy monstrosity of a hotel ever again!"

He zips up his jeans and lets out a deep sigh. "This wasn't supposed to happen. It could hurt you, Tali. It could kill you."

I fight the hot tears building behind my eyes, refusing to give him the satisfaction of seeing me break down. He doesn't deserve these tears. And I hate that I let him in close enough to warrant them. "I don't want to hear any more of your bullshit. It means nothing to me. *You* mean nothing to me." I poke him hard in the chest. "You. Mean. Nothing!" And then for good measure, I grasp his bandaged ear and squeeze with every sliver of strength in me. His face pales and he lets out a bloodcurdling scream, his hand flying up to cover it.

I smirk and tie up the ends of my blouse since all of the buttons are scattered across the floor. "Now you know how I feel right now." I push back my hair and wipe under my eyes, ready to face the world after having my heart shattered yet again.

I need stronger barricades next time.

Barbed and electrified wire.

Nobody will get close ever again.

A voice from within the depths of my mind makes my gut clench.

You don't deserve to be happy.

You've taken it away from too many people.

You can't be redeemed.

You will only suffer for your sins.

A sob gets caught in the back of my throat as I pull open the office door. I can't look back at Cristian. It doesn't matter what I see, anyway. I can't trust his eyes or his expressions. I can't trust anything he says or does.

I can't trust him, period.

He challenged my first instincts about him, made me take a chance.

Several chances.

It was a risk. A big risk on so many levels.

I thought I'd been wrong about him, *hoped* I'd been wrong.

After this morning, he showed me a different side. One I liked. One I thought I could love.

God, I was dead wrong.

And now that I know the truth about who and what he really is...

Well, I can't very well just bury myself in a hole and let him get away with it, can I?

No.

I *can't*.

Chapter Eighteen
CRISTIAN

I collapse into a chair after Tali storms out of the office, my shoulders slumping forward. What the hell did I just do?

I caused myself even more of a shit load of trouble, that's for sure.

Christ only knows what Alek will do to me when he finds out.

I wince, shifting so that my injured arm isn't pressed against the chair. Not that the pain is anything compared to the deep ache in my heart.

I didn't come to Monaco for any reason other than to find out who killed Dad and Daniel Tava. That was my objective. And somehow, against every rule I'd set for myself, Tali managed to creep under my skin.

And because of that, I screwed up. Again. Put myself and my family in danger.

I still don't have answers.

But dammit, I have something else...something I never planned on ever having again since I've seen firsthand what they can do to you and people you love when you least expect it.

Feelings. Gooey, romantic feelings for a woman who has the tongue of a viper and the body of a porn star.

Not something a mafia hit man likes to admit to.

Feelings make you do stupid shit without thinking about consequences. They fuck with your mind, make you lose sight of your responsibilities and goals. They derail you from doing your job.

And, they can get you killed.

That's the part I seem to keep forgetting.

I clench my fist and rub it against my temple. I could have gotten iced the other night after I left the beach because I was focused on *her*.

I need to shift that focus, or else a bum shoulder will be the least of my injuries.

If I'm not careful, I'll end up just like Dad and Daniel.

I struggle to my feet and pull open the office door. I can't sit in there forever, avoiding the storm I've just invited into my life. I don't bother buttoning my shirt. It takes too much time and effort, and right now, I don't have the energy to spare.

I need to find the killer. Killers. What the fuck ever.

The ones who turned shit upside down.

Even if Alek wasn't completely full of shit, even if he was trying to throw me off, the reality is that there are people on the hunt for me.

I don't know if they're his people or someone else's people, but they're coming.

Soon.

I tug at the ends of my hair, gritting my teeth as I stagger back into the lobby. The hairs on the back of my neck prickle as I replay our mainly one-sided conversation in my head. Why would Alek tell me Tava sold him his portion of the shipping business? Especially if he knows I'm a target for the same people who killed Tava? Wouldn't he be worried I'd sell him out if they got too close to me?

Unless...

My iPhone pings, and I pull it out of my pocket to see what the hell is about to go sideways.

Because a nagging feeling tells me I lost my focus again, and this time it's going to cost me.

A lot.

I frown at the screen. It's from Jak. He's bringing a *guest*.

Good Christ. Does that mean—?

"Cristian!" Diego's voice bellows, startling me from my thoughts. "Where the hell have you been?"

"I went to talk to Alek Severinov, just like I said I would."

"You've been gone for a long time." He narrows his eyes. "Is that all you were doing?"

"Yeah," I mumble, leaning over one of the computers. I tap the keyboard, bringing up a local news site. Anything to avoid his critical eyes.

"And what did you find out?"

I scrub a hand down the front of my face. "Let's just say I got a lot more out of him than I expected."

"What the hell does that mean?"

Tires screech to a halt outside the clear glass revolving door, and Jak jumps out of his black Mercedes SLX. He stalks to the back of the car and pops open the trunk.

Diego and I run outside. It's not a coincidence that my hotel is located at the very bottom of a steep hill, the front lobby completely invisible to nosy eyes. It's also what helps me keep it so 'exclusive.' As in, hosting a very limited number of guests. Me, Diego, Jak, the Doc, and my security team.

"Oh, shit," I grunt when he holds up his hand. "What the fuck is in there, Jak?"

"Not what," he says with a grimace. "But *who*."

I push past Diego and peer into the trunk, running a hand through my hair. "Fuuuck."

"Do I even want to know?" Diego groans, collapsing into one of the decorative benches lining the cobblestone driveway.

I shake my head. "Get him out of there and inside. *Fast*."

I pull Diego up by the collar and drag him inside with me. "Listen, we don't have a lot of time, so here's what I know. Alek Severinov told me Daniel Tava agreed to sell him his portion of the shipping business. This happened right before Tava was killed in that hit-and-run. He claims the people looking for us are also going to be looking for whoever owns Tava's share in that business. But nobody knows it's the Severinovs. Yet."

"So…" Diego paces in front of the reception desk. "Right now, we're the only ones being targeted."

"Alek claims someone killed Tava to keep the news of the Severinovs owning that share quiet."

"But why? I don't get it, Cristian. What the hell am I missing?"

"I don't know." I tap my fingers on the desk. "Let's see what this douchebag has to say. Maybe he can help us connect the dots. Jak picked him up for a reason."

Jak grunts as he drags Michel Dubois, the scumbag land surveyor, through the front door of my hotel. He's had a pretty rough few days, starting with Tali sterilizing him at the gala and breaking his wrist for good measure. Then, judging from the blood and bruises on Dubois's face, Jak encountered a bit of the French resistance when he was trying to get some answers out of him.

The fact that he's here and still alive tells me Jak's interrogation didn't go swimmingly.

"Tell them what you told me," Jak growls in Dubois's face.

With wide, terrified eyes, he shakes his head, his voice muffled.

I roll my eyes and pull off the duct tape from his lips.

He screams like a bitch.

Hmm.

Pretty much what I expected.

"Speak!" I glare at him, folding my arms across my chest. "Next time, I won't ask so fucking nicely." I am so tired of this shit. Chasing my tail only to find someone I thought I might be able to trust is just another low-life asshole on the take.

Why is that so surprising?

He'd probably suck cock for money, scumbag that he is.

Tears spill from Michel's eyes, and I turn away to yell at Jak and Diego. "Are you fucking kidding me? Are we really going to believe anything this pussy has to say? He can't even speak, for fuck's sake! Get him inside!" I go to the front door and lock it behind us.

Just in case.

You just never know, and even with all of the security cameras feeding me data, it never hurts to be on the safe side.

Jak lifts an eyebrow when I return and drags Michel into the office where I'd just nailed Tali only minutes earlier. Diego and I follow close behind. I pull a roll of duct tape out of a drawer and tape his wrists and feet together. Jak slams another drawer shut and holds up a knife and a set of pliers, daring him to remain quiet.

"I know who killed Daniel Tava!"

I nod. "Now we're getting somewhere. Give me a name."

"I c-can't."

I look at Jak. "Seriously? This is the result of your in-depth investigation?"

Jak rolls his eyes. "I was gonna kill him, but then I figured it was too much like your MO. You know, when you kill a guy without finding out whom he works for?"

Diego snickers as he lounges against a desk, taking in the show.

"Fuck you, Jak." I lean down so I'm staring Michel in the face. "Poor baby. You look like you're about to shit your pants. Am I right?"

He keeps whimpering and nodding his head. "P-p-please don't hurt me!"

"Then why won't you tell me what I want to know? I want a name!" I yell as Jak approaches with the pliers. He grabs one of Michel's hands and closes them on one of his fingers, just tight enough. I smirk as Michel squeals like a pig. "Imagine how it's gonna feel when we snip off your shriveled little dick!"

"Ahh!" He screams again when Jak applies a little pressure to his finger for the second time. "No!"

"If he squeezes it a third time, you can bet that finger is gonna be on the floor!" Diego yells, getting up and launching a punch at his jaw.

Michel is full-on bawling right now, blood oozing from the corner of his mouth. Christ Almighty. What in the hell led Jak to this pansy-ass in the first place?

"We're wasting time," I hiss, turning away from them. "If he's working for someone, we need to find out who now. Not later, but right fucking now!" I yank open a tall cabinet and pull out a gun. I cock it and hold it right between Michel's beady, black eyes. A large stain slowly bleeds into the groin area of his khakis. I bend down. "Oh, yeah. We're doing this my way now. I don't give a flying fuck about your fingers. Or your dick. I want the information you have inside of that pea-sized brain, and if it doesn't come out of your mouth on the count of three, it will be all over the fucking walls!" I press the gun hard against his skull. "You pissed yourself, so you know I mean what I say. The choice is yours, fucker. You tell me the name, and I'll spare your ass."

I cock the gun. "One...

Michel starts hyperventilating. He writhes in the chair, begging and pleading for his life.

"Two..."

The tears start up again, and Diego joins in the festivities. "Hey, Michel. You know we're gonna go after your wife and son after this, right? They're next on the list if you don't cooperate."

More blubbering and all of the *please, please, please* bullshit follows. I can't take this crap anymore.

"Three!"

He opens his mouth and screams the name I've been waiting for.

"Tali Severinov!"

I clench my teeth. "Liar!" I scream in his face.

Crack!

One shot between the eyes and Michel slumps over in the chair, brain splattered everywhere.

Exactly as promised.

Chapter Nineteen

TALI

Tears blur my vision as I drive toward Destination: Nowhere. I've tried calling Alek three times since leaving Cristian's hotel, but each one goes straight to voicemail.

And that damn voice taunts me again and again.

You'll never be happy, Tali...

I slam my fist on the steering wheel and let out a shriek of the windshield-shattering variety. I walked right into his trap, yet again. He doesn't want me. He never did.

And him giving me that land — why? There must be something wrong with it. It must have issues, because a selfish, self-centered bastard like Cristian Marcone doesn't just do nice things for people without having an agenda of his own.

It's not like he gave it to me because he actually gives a shit about why it's so important to me.

"Motherfucker!" I scream as the seascape flies by in my periphery. Why did I run out of his hotel so quickly? I should have stayed. I should have showed him what it feels like to have your heart ripped out of your chest because you've made yet another horrific choice.

I made one with Alain.

And now this.

At least Cristian isn't blackmailing me.

But he deserves a major ass-kicking anyway.

I swallow hard, swiping at the tears streaming down my face. "I'm tired of being this person!" I screech, gripping the steering wheel tight. "I need to take my life back, goddammit!"

I wasn't planning a pit stop, but something led me to this place. It's led me here more times than I can count over the past few weeks. I swing the Escalade off the road, tires squealing on the pavement right at the sharp curve, right where my life became Alain's.

When it became his.

I get out of the truck and slam the door shut. I run my finger along the shiny, black hood as I walk around the front, the paint glittering under the hot sun.

Just a couple of weeks ago, my car was cherry red.

A cherry red Maserati.

I haven't seen it since that night with Alain.

He'd gone to a party to host some business clients. Or at least, that's the bullshit story he'd fed me. But I knew better and was tired of being humiliated by his cheating ass. I'd put up with it for long enough because I'd been vulnerable, and lonely.

Then something inside me snapped, unleashing months of wrath, anger, and pain.

It was the wake-up call I needed to take back my life and eliminate the toxin otherwise known as Alain Leclercq.

But my God, I wish I'd never driven myself to that party to catch him in the act! I wish I'd never seen Alain dry humping that sleazy whore in the corner. I wish I'd have just stayed home, watched television, gone for a run, done anything other than what I actually did.

I wish, I wish, I wish…

And it never does any good. I never wake up from the nightmares. They haunt me twenty-four-seven.

I can't change what happened.

What I allowed to happen.

There is no redo option.

It's just game over.

I lie back on the grass next to the side of the road, flinging an arm over my eyes to shield them from the bright sun.

But that's the problem with closing my eyes and retreating into my toxic thoughts.

The sights and sounds come rushing back from the dark corners of my mind, consuming me like a deadly tsunami, the force whipping me in all directions, pummeling me until I can no longer claw my way to the surface.

I always succumb.

I clench my fists.

Always…

I stagger and sway out the door of the club, still screaming at Alain who is right on my heels. He tries to grab my wrist, but I twist his fingers back until he yelps for mercy.

"You've made a fool of me for the last time, you two-timing prick bastard!"

"Tali, stop! You're in no condition to drive!" Alain reaches for me again, clearly thinking that the booze has impacted my ability to fuck his shit up beyond repair.

Somewhere in my memories, there is a sea of curious faces in my view. Wide-eyed, nosy assholes. Haven't they ever seen a cheating bastard get kicked to the curb by his scorned girlfriend?

"Get the fuck off of me!" I scream, pulling open the door of my cherry red Maserati. "I never want to see you again!"

Again, he tries to catch my wrist, but I turn and throw an elbow with all of the force I can muster, the bone connecting right with his nose. Blood immediately pours out of his nostrils and all over his Armani suit, and I allow myself a triumphant smile.

"That's my final word, you asshole!" I slide into the driver's seat and press the button to start the ignition. Lights flash across my eyes, everything a blur. But I don't care. I need to get away from him, away from the humiliation that he's caused me.

I did this to myself. I let him get the upper hand because I was lonely.

I thought he was a good guy, a genuine guy.

I should have seen the signs.

But I missed them...all of them.

I switch gears, putting the car in Drive, when the passenger side door opens. Alain jumps into the seat and puts his hand over mine. "I'm not letting you drive like this! You're going to get yourself killed!"

"I hate you!" I scream, tears spilling out of my eyes. "Just stay here with your slut ass friends! I don't want you in my life, Alain! It's over!"

"Don't say that," he says, his voice husky, his hand still on top of mine. "It was just a misunderstanding, Tali. There wasn't anything going on.

You've been drinking, baby. You were seeing things that weren't there."

"Oh, so I didn't actually see your hand up her skirt? That was just the alcohol making me hallucinate?" I yank my hand away from his. "Get out of my car!"

"We can get past this. Please. Give me another chance. I can't live without you. I want to marry you and start a family—"

My shoulders quake, my fingertips numb from gripping the steering wheel so tight. "You had me and you threw me away in front of the entire fucking world!" I turn toward him and shove him into the passenger side door. Unfortunately, it's closed so he doesn't fall out onto the pavement, and I can't run him over.

"Listen, let's just go home and talk about this, okay? Don't throw away what we have."

"You already did that!" I shriek. "Now get out of my—"

A clicking sound makes me blink fast. I recoil. Fuck no, tell me I'm hallucinating again...

Alain's dark, deep-set eyes narrow, a murderous glare lurking in the depths.

"Since I couldn't talk any sense into you, maybe this will help."

A sharp pain slices into my side as the hard metal tip of Alain's gun presses into my skin. My breath stills, my heart galloping out of control. "What the hell is this? What are you doing?"

"We've been here for too long. Now, take your foot off the brake and drive this fucking car, Natalya," he hisses.

I swallow hard, wincing as he keeps the tip pressed into me. I ease my foot off the brake and drive, my temples thundering as blood rushes between them. I shouldn't be driving. If I'd have just called a car, this wouldn't be happening!

Oh, God, what even is happening?

I peer into the rearview mirror, praying that a cop jumps out from behind a bush and pulls me over. I'd happily accept a DUI arrest right now if it would get me away from this crazy bastard. I drive slowly because I am a hot mess right now, but the thought does cross my mind that by driving into a tree, I can get the hell away from him and from whatever he's plotting in his evil mind.

The tip digs deeper, and I let out a squeal. "Please, stop! Why are you doing this?"

"No, you stop," he says, peering at the dark road behind us. We're far enough away from the club that it's completely out of sight. "You're too plastered to be driving. Get out of the car. I'm taking over."

"The fuck you will!" Colors and shapes swim in front of my eyes, and if I had any shot of escaping, it was probably before I had that last shot at the bar. Everything spins, and I clutch the sides of my head to hold everything steady so I can think.

Plan.

Pray.

Alain gets out and runs over to my side, pulling open the door. He grabs me by the arm and yanks me out of the seat. Then he walks me over to the other side of the car and throws me into the passenger seat. The sudden jerking motion makes bile rise in my throat, and I double over, emptying the contents of my stomach at my feet.

Alain doesn't say a word. He straps himself into the seat and tells me to do the same.

Odd. If he wanted me dead, would he care whether or not I'm wearing a seatbelt?

He keeps the gun pointed at me as he drives, weaving around steep curves as we head in the direction of the Prince's palace.

I try to make sense of the direction he's headed, but my skull is pounding and it hurts to think.

He picks up speed, cornering the roads like the tires are on rails. I clutch the sides of the leather seat, my heart lodged in my throat. The urge to scream is so powerful, but if I open my mouth again, I know exactly what will happen.

And a scream won't be the only thing that emerges.

But after a few agonizing minutes, I can no longer keep quiet. He's approaching a blind curve, but he doesn't slow down. He goes faster and faster as he takes the turn, almost as if he's trying to plow my car into the side of the cliff. "Slow down, you asshole! You're going too fast! We're going to cra—!"

The scent of searing metal against rock as the car plows into something hard makes my stomach roll. I'm thrust forward upon impact, my head cracking against the dashboard. The nausea which had gripped me only seconds earlier is quickly replaced with blackness as my eyes droop closed.

When they drift open, I have no idea who much time has passed. I rub the front of my head and there is already a growing lump by my hairline. My vision blurs as I peer out of the cracked windshield. I can't see anything through the spider web of crushed glass. "Alain?" I whisper, turning my head to find an empty driver's seat. I slowly look out the window and gasp, my hand flying to my mouth.

This time, I might really need to keep it closed.

A gagging sensation assaults me, and I push open the door, dry heaving with my head hanging out of the car. I crumble to the pavement, crawling over to Alain...

And the motionless body of the person he just hit.

"Oh my God, oh my God," I whimper as I approach the bloody and mangled mess of a man on the side of the road. "Is he...?"

"Yeah," Alain grunts, pulling out his phone and walking away, speaking in fast French to whoever is on the other line.

He must be talking to emergency services. Or the police. Someone who can help. Someone who will know what to do!

I reach out, my fingers tentatively grazing the man's cold and lifeless hand. What if he has a family? A wife? Children? They'll be so worried. So wracked with grief when they find out that he's gone from their lives forever.

A sob escapes from deep in my throat, remembering the pain of losing my own mother and father. God, what if his children are young? Just babies? What if—?

"Get up. We're leaving."

I look up at Alain and furrow my brow. "What are you doing?" *I whisper through my tears.* "We can't leave. He'll be all by himself!"

"He won't know the difference," *Alain growls.* "We have to get out of here."

"You can't be serious!" *I press my hand to my temples, praying that the Earth stops spinning before I crumble to my knees.*

"I am. Deadly serious." *The corners of his thin lips curl up into a sinister smirk. Like he's amused at his own joke.*

"You just ran over and killed an innocent man! I'm not leaving! I'm staying right here! It's the right thing to do!"

"Oh, yeah?" *He sneers, holding the gun right against my forehead with one hand and fisting my hair with the other.* "Well, let me tell you my opinion. This man made his fucking bed. And he sure as hell doesn't deserve to sleep in it."

"You know who this is?"

"Tali, Tali, Tali," *He taps the gun against his own cheek.* "So beautiful, yet stupid. Yes, I know who it is. And yes, I made it look like an accident. But make no mistake. When I want the truth to come out, I will. And it will not be an accident at all."

My brain is so fuzzy from the excess of alcohol that I don't follow his sick and twisted path of thought. "But it wasn't an accident...why would you let the authorities think it is and then come out and tell the truth?"

He laughs, a wicked, demonic laugh that curdles my blood. "I wouldn't do that, my love. I'm not a fucking idiot."

"But how...why..." I shake my head, instantly regretting it since it makes my gut clench again. "This doesn't make any sense to me."

"Let me clarify things for you, then, okay?" He steps forward, holding up his phone. One by one, the pictures slide by my eyes...me outside of the club looking like the hot mess I am, me in the driver's seat of my car, me bent over the body, grazing the man's cold and lifeless hand as tears spill down my face.

I gasp. "You bastard," I hiss, reaching out a hand and grabbing for the phone. He pulls it away so fast, I stumble forward into him.

"Yeah, that's about right."

"Nobody will believe you!" I yell, backing away from him toward the road. "Help! Help!" I scream, waving my hands in the air.

My angry, slurring voice is amplified as Alain raises the volume on his phone. My threats. My belligerence when he begs me to hand over my car keys.

When the hell did he even take those videos?

And how blitzed am I that I didn't notice?

"There are a hundred witnesses that saw you leave in a drunken haze tonight. And they watched you get into your car and drive in the direction of the 'accident.' Oh, but there's more," he says, walking toward me, the gun steady and pointed right at me. "You even think about going to your brothers about this, and I will make sure that this man's enemies know exactly who drove into him tonight. That is going to make these people very angry because he owed them a lot of money, money they will never collect." He leans in close, the stench of stale whiskey on his breath.

"They will come for you. Money won't appease them, Tali. And they won't just stop at you. They will take out your whole fucking family. Do you understand?"

My breaths come in short and sharp gasps. "You...you...sadistic bastard!"

He nods. "Sadistic. Brilliant. What the fuck ever. The bottom line is, I win. I own you now." He flashes his malicious smile once again. "Now, how's that for having the last word?"

I sit straight up, my eyes flying open when I hear my iPhone ring on the passenger's seat. Maybe it's Alek. Maybe he can help me figure out a way out of this. Christ, I don't even know who I'm fighting. That night is such a blur, and after the news plastered the story on every media outlet in the freaking world hours later...when I found out who we killed and who his enemies actually are...a chill zips through me just thinking about it.

I'm not so sure Alek can save me and the rest of our family.

But I have to try. I have to grab back some of the control I've lost. I need to make this right.

For a lot of people.

Justice must be served, and if I go down, so be it.

I just need to protect my family.

They're the only people I have in this world, a fact that Cristian made painfully clear to me less than an hour ago.

I struggle to my feet and jog over to my car, pulling open the passenger door and grabbing the phone just as a line of blacked-out SUVs barrels up the road, spitting up dirt and gravel as they surround the Escalade.

And me.

The cars are unmarked, and I back away, clutching the phone that has now stopped ringing. My eyes dart left and right. Cops?

Could someone have figured out what we did? Are they here to arrest me? Why hasn't anyone jumped out to cuff me?

I spin around and run toward the staircase hidden in the side of the cliff, the same one Cristian jumped from that night he got his ear bitten off.

By birds.

My feet scramble to make it up the steps, but before I can blink, men dressed in head-to-toe black appear and leap at me as I claw my way up the side of the rock.

"No, no, no!" I scream as they pull me off the steps and I crash to the ground, my head cracking against a large boulder. Images swim in front of my eyes, faces and bodies one big blur. I am suddenly very aware of my heartbeat which thuds, echoing harshly between my temples.

A hand pulls me up to a sitting position and I squint, trying to make out the person who is helping me up.

My chest tightens.

Alain.

He's smiling, and suddenly, I wish I'd have just been knocked out from the impact of my head slamming against the rock. I don't want to see what comes next, what path I chose for my life when I let Alain Leclercq slither his snake ass into my bed.

Bile rises in my throat and I don't try to hold it back. Alain holds back my hair as my retching ensues. Only when my body calms itself does he actually speak.

"It's time, Tali."

"Time for what?" I ask, croaking the words through wads of imaginary cotton.

My ringtone blares, my phone vibrating against my hand. Alain yanks it out of my grasp, and I roll away, scurrying a path through the goons crowding me. They grab me by my hair and clap a hand over my mouth. I kick at my assailants, throwing myself backward for leverage and pounding on whoever comes close. I bite down hard on the fingers pressed against my lips. I scream and curse through the beefy hand, but everything is muffled.

Muted.

Exactly the way Alain wanted me.

"Alek," he says in a smooth voice. "What great timing. Your sister and I are about to host a little party at my place. We have a very special announcement to make. Oh, and feel free to bring a friend or two. The more, the merrier. And...deadlier."

I thrust my body to the left, elbowing one of the assholes whose hand is clamped over my mouth. He lets out a loud groan and loosens his grip enough that I can pry it away from my lips.

"Alek, no! Stay away! It's a trap!" I scream as loud as I can, praying he can hear me.

One of the goons punches me in the jaw, and I crumble to my knees, holding the side of my face.

Oh, yeah. I see stars now.

Alain bends down, grins at me, holds up the phone so I can hear Alek's panicked voice through the speaker, and ends the call.

"Click."

Chapter Twenty
CRISTIAN

"I think this is a big fucking mistake. You don't know what the hell you're walking into, Cristian, " Diego growls, accelerating around a turn as we drive toward the Hermitage Hotel.

Alek's hotel.

"I need answers." I stab his phone number onto the keyboard and wait for him to answer. Ring, ring, ring...and nothing. Same for Tali. And my nerves are stretched to the point where I'm gonna snap like a fucking rubber band at any second.

"I think we already got a pretty big clue about who's conspiring against us from Michel Dubois right before you blew his fucking head off. What the hell makes you so sure that he's wrong? Is it because you're too pussy-whipped to admit that you...once again...didn't think with the head on your one good shoulder?"

"I told you. Tali didn't kill Tava! It's bullshit!" I dial again, my throat tight.

"And what makes you so sure? Because she didn't pull a gun on you after you fucked her? You think your cock alone made her change her mind about the Severinov family's grand plan to wipe us off the map?" Diego doesn't move his eyes from the road in front of him, but I know if he turned his head, daggers would fly out and slice my head in two.

"What?" An angry voice barks into the phone when Alek finally picks up.

I let out the breath I've been holding. "It's Marcone. We need to talk. *Now*."

"I don't have time for you or your bullshit right now, Marcone."

Diego swerves around a turn and pulls into the driveway at the hotel. "I just pulled up to your hotel. Make the time."

"I'm not there, asshole."

I furrow my brow and motion for Diego to stop the car. "Where are you? And where's Tali?"

"I'm taking care of business. Family business. And it's none of yours, Marcone."

"Look, I don't have the patience to play Twenty fucking Questions with you, Alek. I just got some information that will be pretty bad for you if it's true."

Alek lets out a frustrated sigh. "I'm down at the Port Fontvielle."

"And Tali?"

"She's been kidnapped."

"By who?" My spine stiffens. "And why?"

"Her boyfriend. Alain Leclercq."

"Why would he kidnap her?"

"I don't know!" Alek yells. "I'm here to find that out, asshole!"

"Are you alone?" I cover the phone with my hand. "Port Fontvielle. Step the fuck on it, Diego."

"Yeah, I came down here as soon as I found out. He's got her for something, and I don't know what. I always knew he was a slimy bastard, but I never thought he'd actually hurt her."

"I'm on my way. Don't do anything until I get there."

I end the call, drop the phone in my lap, and scrub a hand down the front of my face. "Some asshole took Tali. Alek said she's been kidnapped."

"By who?"

"Her boyfriend."

"Does that really qualify as kidnapping or just really kinky foreplay?"

"Alain Leclercq," I mumble, ignoring Jak's question. "Who the hell is he?"

"Power player here in Monaco and back in France. He originally came from Corsica," Jak says as Diego drives back toward the shore. "He pulled a lot of shit years ago, stole a lot of money from some pretty badass people his dad used to work for. I'd heard he was looking to edge them out so he could take control of their empire. But they found out and had his father killed. Leclercq decided it was time to pick up the vendetta, so he slowly yanked away more and more of their power until he had almost everything."

"Jesus, did you watch a documentary on the guy?" Diego asks.

"Look, I read, okay? You should try it sometime. It'll help you learn some big boy words." Jak snipes. "He and your girl...who should have never become your girl, by the way... have been all over the news since they started dating. Leclercq is a real scumbag and the world knows it. Too bad Tali didn't figure it out sooner."

"Maybe she already had. Maybe that's why he took her in the first place. Maybe he didn't like that she was ready to walk away," I say. "But why?"

"Maybe he's got something on her," Jak responds in a matter-of-fact voice.

I press my fingertips to my temples as Diego pulls into the parking lot of the desolate port. This isn't the main port for Monaco. It's more secluded. Private. Free from prying eyes.

Which is great because I have a feeling a lot of bad shit is about to go down here.

"Okay, where are you gonna find Alek Severinov, Cristian?"

A small sedan swerves around our car and screeches to a halt next to a Range Rover. It's the only other cars in the parking lot. Two men jump out, and I narrow my eyes, recognizing one of them. It's Tali's dickhead brother, Kaz.

The second guy is just as tall but leaner. And they both run over to the Range Rover. The driver's side door opens, and Alek steps out.

Bingo.

"Pull in next to them," I say to Diego, and my feet are on the concrete before he can press the brakes.

"What the hell is happening, Alek?" I stalk over to the three men. "I just blew the fucking head off of Michel Dubois because he told me Tali is the one who killed Daniel Tava."

"What the hell are you talking about?' Kaz pushes against me with his broad chest. "Our sister didn't kill anyone!"

Alek rubs the back of his neck. "Relax, Kaz. Stand down for one second, goddammit!" He turns to me. "I told you whoever did it would be hunted by everyone who was owed money by Tava.

Why the hell would Tali want to sic the international underworld on her own family?"

"Listen, I hate to break up this party, but here's a thought. Maybe we get her back and ask her? How about that?" Diego says, rolling his eyes.

"I don't trust you," I say to Alek.

"I don't trust you, either," he says, his teeth clenched.

"That's fair." I nod. "But I am in love with your sister, and fuck me if I shouldn't have trusted her, either. I need to know the truth and we need to help each other."

Alek stares at me for a few seconds.

"We can handle this just fine on our own," Kaz growls.

"No, he comes, too," Alek says, pointing at a large yacht at the end of the row. "That's Leclercq's boat. Where he stays when he's not shacking up with my sister." He sees my pinched expression and backpedals. "Sorry."

I shrug. "Are we just gonna storm the place?" I shield my eyes and stare at the boat. "They're waiting. They know you're coming."

"Yeah, but they'll never expect *this* crew," Kaz mutters, palming the gun in the back of his jeans. He looks at Alek. "Thank fuck we were able to get off that plane. It was almost ready to take off. I've been waiting for a year to blow a hole into that fucking frog and I'd have been pissed off if I missed my chance."

I look around. The whole area is exposed. Everyone standing on the dock is a target.

Leclercq's guys are definitely watching. They have to know we're here.

But for some reason, nobody is shooting.

"There are two guards on top, standing watch," the other guy...I assume another brother...says, pointing. Fortunately, both of those yahoos are staring at their phones. Real tight security detail.

"Leo, cover the left side. Kaz, you cover the right." Alek nods at Jak and Diego next. "Whoever you guys are, back them up. Cristian and I will go after Leclercq. He wants me on that boat. He has something to tell me and he wants me to hear it before he tries to kill me. The rest of you are collateral damage in his eyes, so pay attention and try hard not to get plugged."

Then he pulls out two guns from the back of his jeans, calmly points at each guard and shoots. The silencers are on, so nobody below deck would have any idea that the boat has already been compromised. The guards, if you can even call them that, both crumble, their phones clattering to the deck. Alek turns to us and nods. "We're clear."

Everything about the guy is cool and unruffled. It's impressive, if I'm being honest. I never know what the hell is going on behind those eyes, but he always seems to have wheels in motion.

I just hope they don't get us derailed.

We creep toward the boat. Kaz climbs up a ladder on the right, and Leo takes the one on the left. They inch around the thin metal rails lining each side of the sleek ship, guns pointed and ready to shoot. I look at Jak and Diego before following Alek over the short gangway to get to the main entrance of the boat. "Alek," I whisper. "Where is everyone? Why aren't they out here?"

He stops short and turns around. "Because he doesn't want me dead. Yet, anyway. He's got Tali for some reason. That's why they made it easy on us getting on the boat in the first place. I knocked off those dipshit guys because I don't want to give us away so soon."

He points his gun at me. "Now listen carefully. I'm gonna say this one time, Marcone. My priority is keeping my family safe. If you or your guys get in my way, I will shoot whoever in the fucking head and not lose a second of sleep over it. Do you understand?"

"Yeah. Same."

He smirks. "Not worried about that part."

I roll my eyes and follow him into the belly of the ship.

Guns drawn, we crouch down low as we approach...what, I have no clue. The blinds are all drawn so we can't see into the main cabin, but there are voices speaking in rapid French.

"I don't suppose you know what they're saying?" I ask Alek as he jogs over toward a closed door, ready to kick it in.

He stares at me, poised with his foot in the air. "They're saying that once they finish us, they're coming for you."

"Well, that's just great. I'm glad I could save them the effort of finding me," I scoff. "Now, can we please destroy these bastards?"

"Back up. I'm going in."

"Wait!" I whisper-shout. "I thought you said Leclercq doesn't want you dead. Why are we busting in?"

"He wants me dead, but on his terms." Alek narrows his eyes. "I only do things on *my* terms, something he's going to learn. Right now!"

Crack!

With one swift kick, the door to the main cabin is thrust open and about ten guys leap to their feet, guns pointed at us. Gunfire explodes into the air as Alek runs in, taking about four of the men out before I have time to blink.

"Now!" Alex bellows.

Glass shatters on either side of the space as Kaz and Leo come flying into the room. I use the opportunity to plug one guy who's standing next to the television. I dive behind one of the couches as glass shatters around me. I point and shoot off a few more rounds, hitting another guy and a lot of the wall next to him. My bad shoulder is aching, but I don't stop. I can't take even a second or—

Suddenly, my body is yanked backward, some fucker fisting a handful of my hair. A whir of his hand puts a knife at my throat, digging into my flesh. I elbow him backward right in the balls to shock him before he's able to slice off my goddamn head. Then I dig my feet into the floor and fling the guy over my head, which is thankfully still attached to the rest of me. A sharp pain explodes down my side, and I clench my teeth. The pain paralyzes me for a split second until I remember that the host of this party still hasn't shown up to greet us.

"Alek, I'm going to find Tali!" I leave the Severinov guys in the main cabin to finish off the rest of Leclercq's army as more appear from other areas of the boat. I duck down a narrow hallway, my breath hitched. Where the hell are Diego and Jak? My gut clenches. *Please don't let them be—*

A door swings open, hitting me square in the nose and sending me flying into a mirrored wall behind me. A husky blond guy jumps out and shoots, but I duck just in enough time for the mirror to explode into tiny shards at my feet.

I hurl a vase of flowers at his head, but he ducks behind the open door before it makes contact. I leap forward, grabbing the door and pounding it into his face. He flies backward, hits the floor, and rolls around to scramble to his feet. More bullets fire, none of them mine, and I dive behind the door, popping my head around to squeeze off a few return shots.

The sound of bullets exploding into the air makes my temples pound. The noxious smell of sulphur assaults my nose, but I keep shooting. More shots pierce the door that I'm huddled behind, and I swing my body against the wall so I can reload.

I pop in a new clip, peek my head around the side of the door again and swallow a groan. Where there was one guy only seconds earlier, now there are about ten more. I don't even know where the hell they came from, but I can only hope Alek and his brothers are close behind.

Otherwise, I'll really be screwed.

A gun barrel presses to the back of my skull, and with a single click, it's cocked and ready to blow my brains out.

I take that back.

I'm pretty badly fucked as it is right now.

Chapter Twenty-One
CRISTIAN

Whoever is behind me yanks me up off the floor and shoves me forward into a bedroom.

The only bedroom with people in it. But just not people.

Tali.

I hit the floor, face-first, cracking my mouth against the leg of the chair.

The chair Tali is tied to, with duct tape slapped over her mouth. The right side of her face is bloody and bruised. I grit my teeth. Where in the fuck are her brothers? And where the hell are Jak and—?

Diego.

Another guy dressed in a black suit pushes him into the room with me and Tali.

I swallow a yelp. At least Tali is alive, which is more than I can say for Diego.

Someone beat the piss out of him and he looks like a goddamn prize fighter right now.

The one who *didn't* win the prize.

Rage bubbles in my veins. When I find the motherfucker who did this to him...

Wait, there's still no sign of Jak.

Shit.

Did they kill him?

I roll over and scramble to my feet, spitting blood. My eyes dart left and right, looking for something...anything I can use to get us out of this place.

No Severinovs, no guns, no fucking chance.

A short, stocky guy with dark blond hair walks into the room. "Cristian Marcone. How lucky am I that you just decided to come along for the ride? I thought I was going to have to send a third team to kill you since the first two underdelivered on my request."

"Who are you?" I growl, breathing heavily, another one of the guards grabbing me by the scruff of my neck.

"I'm the host of this little soiree, of course." He says this in a heavy French accent and I know immediately who it is.

Alain Leclercq. French fucker.

"What have you done with the Severinovs?"

"I should think you'd be more concerned about what I'm going to do to you, Mr. Marcone." He inches closer in his expensive suit and shoes. I want to tear this bastard in half right now, and if I didn't think I'd get shot in the head as a result, I'd lunge for his puny ass. "Now that I have you here, make no mistake. You won't be a returning guest."

I catch a glimpse of Tali in my periphery and her shoulders shake, her eyes brimming with tears.

"Untie her. Let her go," I grunt, breathing heavily, still searching for a weapon of any kind...and coming up empty.

"You see, I just can't do that right now. She's too valuable to me. As are you."

"What do you want?"

"Well," he says, tapping a finger against his chin. "Let's see. I wanted a lot to start. I did. I'll admit it. I'm a greedy bastard," he says, chuckling. He sweeps a hand over Tali's head and captures her chin in his hand. "I always was, though, wasn't I?"

She shrugs his hand off of her and he takes the back of his hand and smacks her across the face. "Stupid bitch. So high maintenance. So damaged. It was only a matter of time before you let me in after your old man died. And once you did..." He shakes his head with a snicker. "It was over. For you and your family."

My chest heaves with the realization that I may be the only one who can save us. Alek, Jak, Kaz, Leo...I have no idea where they are and Diego is half-conscious at this point.

"What the hell are you talking about? Why is Tali here?"

Leclercq looks at me, a surprised smirk on his smug face. "I really wanted you to connect the dots yourself, Marcone. It would have been so much more fun to see that happen than to have to explain it all to you. But, if I must...well, I'd rather do it when our other guest of honor shows up."

I struggle against the asshole holding my arms so tight behind my back that they are damn close to snapping in two. Leclercq steps closer and leans in toward me. "And as a little teaser for you, let me just say you and Alek Severinov together under one roof excites me more than a fucking porn star excites a teenaged boy."

I try to yank my arms out of this asshole's grip to no avail. And this time, he's not putting up with my shit, either. With a strike to the side of my face, I crash to the floor next to my brother. I groan, holding the part of my face that I think just shattered when that punch pummeled me to the floor. I'm trying so hard to make sense of this shit and failing miserably. And with this crack to the head, my brain is too damn fuzzy to process any more right now.

"Ah! Here we go!" Leclercq stands up from the chair. "Guest of honor number two." He walks past Tali and yanks her hair backward. "I'm actually glad you decided to fuck around behind my back, Princess. If you hadn't, I'd have had more work to do to kill Marcone. But now that I have him *and* your brother in the same place and at the same time? Well, life if just pretty fucking perfect for me."

I squint at the doorway and see Alek's pinched face as he's shoved into the room.

Alek drops next to me and my eyes flicker up at the person who delivered him to the enemy. At least, the person I *thought* was our collective enemy.

I press my fingertips to my temples and squeeze my eyes closed. It can't be. It cannot fucking be!

Jak.

His dark eyes, focused on my face with a harsh glare.

My blood turns to ice, my heart thundering against my chest. The urge to lunge at him like a rabid dog and tear him apart with my fingers is so strong, but I stand down.

For the moment.

"You motherfucker," I hiss at him.

"Gotcha," he says with that nasty smirk.

"What are you doing, Jak? Do you really want to go head to head with me?"

"Doesn't really look like it'll be much of a fight, Cristian." He drops to one knee next to me. "I have your balls in a vise. And guess what? After I crush them, I'm going to make a shit ton on the deal."

"My father made you what you are today! He gave you so much, you ungrateful bastard! You were his right hand for so long. How could you—?"

He lets out a dry chuckle. "Yes, I was. And he trusted me with plenty, fucking idiot that he was. He never realized a thing. None of you did. And it served me very well over the years. I made a hell of a lot off of him. Met a lot of very enterprising people who wanted to reward me for my work."

Alain gets up and joins in the sinister laughter. He passes Tali and pulls the tape off her mouth with one swipe. She screams, and he laughs at her. "Princess, nobody who can hear you gives a flying fuck, so please just stop."

"Alek," Tali whimpers, her voice quivering. "It was Alain who killed Daniel Tava. He's been blackmailing me since it happened."

Alek lets out a groan and it seems like he connects the dots as soon as he hears that.

I wish I could say the same for myself.

"I knew that slimy bastard Tava sold you his shares of the shipping company," Leclercq snarls in Alek's face. "But nobody else does, luckily for me. I also knew that you'd do anything to protect your baby sister if big bad me threatened to out her to the world, to all of your new enemies...the people who Tava owned a shit ton of money to. Including *me*." He holds up his phone. "The proof would have fucked you all beyond recognition."

"So what do you want, Leclercq?" Alek asks. "My shares?"

"And Marcone's." He smirks. "I want it all!"

"And you think that's what's gonna get you what you're looking for? Power, an empire to run? You think money is all it takes, you dumb fuck?" He drags himself to his feet, leaning his tall frame over Leclercq.

"No," Alain says, puffing out his chest and trying to pull himself up so that he isn't dwarfed by Alek. "It takes a loyal group of people, too. And how do you find them? Well, all you need to do is find out who was screwed over by your enemies. Show them your strength, promise them you can make their troubles disappear, make them back what they lost tenfold, and suddenly, they're on your team, pledging undying loyalty. That's how I know none of Tava's debtors will come after me. Once I have control of that shipping company, I'll be too valuable to them. But there are some people who don't care about money. They care about revenge and will stand by the one who can help them get it. Just like your *friend*, Jak Scala here. He practically delivered you to me on a silver platter after you blew away Michel Dubois, Marcone."

Alain sighs. "I hated to use Michel like bait since he served such great purpose. But life is all about making the tough decisions."

Jak glowers at me. "Your father made a big mistake when he picked me to be his number two after killing my family. But you made a bigger mistake when you murdered my sister, Maria, the only person I had left in the world! That's the one you're about to pay for."

I leap to my feet and jump at Jak, tackling him to the floor. I swing my fists with every ounce of strength I have, and if someone shoots me, so be it. I won't let this traitorous bastard get away with betraying my family.

I crawl on top of him, pounding my fist into his face. "You motherfucker! You set me up! You set all of us up!"

One of Leclercq's other guys pulls me off of him and drags me to a corner of the room.

"I told you to be careful, Cristian. That your anger and rage were eventually going to fuck you up." Jak rolls to his feet and leans over Diego's near-motionless body. He pulls out a knife and jams it into Diego's side with a triumphant laugh. "It's like déjà fucking vu, huh, Cristian? What are you gonna do? You couldn't save your father after I plugged him full of lead. Do you even have it in you to save your brother?"

"No," I yell, leaping at Jak and digging my fingers into his neck. I can barely breathe because my throat is so damn tight.

If we don't get him help, Diego's gonna bleed out right here.

Gunshots erupt down the hallway and heavy thumping tells me the threat of an impending death trap has quadrupled. I slam Jak's head into the floor, over and over again, wondering why nobody has taken a shot at me. Bullets explode into the air around me, and I pause for a second when I hear yelling in Russian.

Kaz and Leo.

They're alive, thank fuck.

"Your sister was a backstabbing bitch and she deserved to die," I seethe. I pull Jak up by the collar, launch my fist back and pound at his temple, once, twice, three times before I let his skull crash to the floor.

Bodies fall to the floor around me like dominoes, and Leclercq's face falls as every one of his guys does the same, thanks to the fact that the rest of the Severinovs have finally showed the fuck up!

Kaz and Leo drop to their knees to untie Tali. I fall to the floor next to my brother.

What are you gonna do? You couldn't save your father.

I dig my phone out of my pocket, my fingers trembling. I need to get the Doc over here as soon as possible or I'll lose Diego. I jab the numbers onto my screen, checking his pulse. He's still alive.

At least for the moment.

"I've got a flat tire," I say when the Doc answers, struggling to keep my voice calm. "I can't drive. I need a new tire right away."

"Okay," he replies. "I'll get the spare."

"You have the location?"

"Yeah, it just came up. I'll be there soon."

I just hope soon is soon enough. I grab sheets off the bed to apply pressure to Diego's side. Memories of that night come rushing back...the night we almost lost Gianna.

The screaming and the blood....Christ, there was so much blood...

I can't lose my brother.

I've already made too many mistakes, ones that put us here in the first place.

My family can't take another loss.

"Guys," I say to Leo and Kaz. "Go wait for the doctor. Keep a watch out for him. And make sure there are no other party guests waiting to join in." My eyes drift to Tali's. "You should go with them. Get somewhere safe."

"No," she whispers. "I'm staying here with you guys."

Kaz and Leo jump up and run out of the room as Alek unleashes all holy hell on Leclercq.

He backs Leclercq into a corner, grabbing him by the throat and pressing his back against a wall. "You stupid asshole. Did you really think you were gonna get away with this? Did you think you had us?"

Leclercq's feet kick around, his face turning a disturbing shade of purple.

"Blackmail, murder, revenge." Alek shakes his head, throwing Leclercq into a door. "Your army...your strong, loyal army. They're all dead. Looks like you hired a lot of second-rate killers, and guess what? You get what you fucking pay for. So now, who's gonna save *you*, Leclercq?"

His fingers graze a gleaming silver serving fork sitting on a table next to the door. He holds it up and looks at it from all angles. "I think I'm gonna keep my half of the company. And I think Marcone is gonna keep his half." He holds out the fork. "But you...you need a parting gift, too. I don't want you to be the only one who walks away with nothing." Alek takes a few steps toward Jak, who is writhing around on the floor after having his head smashed in. He fists Jak's hair and pulls him to a sitting position, turning to Leclercq. "I want you to watch this very carefully, okay? Because it is nothing compared to what I'm going to do to you."

He takes a breath, and without even blinking, he shoves the fork into Jak's eye, dragging it down the side of his face. Alek's jaw twitches, the corners of his lips creeping upward as Leclercq cries like a bitch in the corner.

Alek smirks at Jak. "And *this* is what I think double crossing bastards like you deserve." He pulls the fork out and slams it right into Jak's cock, through the fabric of his jeans.

My ears are numb from the screams that follow.

Suddenly, Leclercq jumps up to grab a gun off the floor a few inches away from him. Alek spins around, as if he sensed the attack was coming. He pulls the fork out of Jak's groin and hurls it at Leclercq, stabbing him right between the eyes.

Out of the corner of my eye, I see a gun that clattered to the floor once Leclercq's army crumbled one by one. I try to kick it over to Alek and miss entirely. I don't even know where it went, but he sure as hell doesn't have it.

Leclercq struggles to his feet, points the gun at Alek and smirks, blood oozing out of the spots where the fork pierced his forehead. "Looks like I'm still taking over your half of the business after all."

"Think again, you motherfucker!"

I twist around to see Tali gripping a gun in her outstretched hand, a murderous glare in her eyes.

The gun.

She fires off three shots to Leclercq's head and chest. He slides down the door, now a bloody red color, and lands on the floor in a heap, his head dropping into his lap. She drops the gun and sinks to her knees next to me.

"That was awesome," I murmur. "You saved your brother's ass."

Alek pulls the fork out of Alain's forehead and walks back over to Jak, twirling the fork in his hands like a baton. "You traitor. We're not done with you. You betrayed your friends and your family. You tried to kill one of your own, and for what?"

Jak moans and whimpers, his body flopping all over the place in a poor attempt to get away from what he knows is coming next.

He just doesn't know how it's gonna happen.

I press the sheet tighter against Diego's wound and lay his head in Tali's lap. She strokes the sides of his pale face...pale aside from the blueish-purple bruises that have formed around his jaw and cheek.

I roll to my feet and grab the fork out of Alek's hand. "I trusted you with my life! With my family's safety! And you've been working against us ever since you set foot into our lives!" I get right in his face and make sure his one eye sees me clearly. "You tried to destroy us!"

"Just like you and your father destroyed me," he gurgles, spitting blood as he grunts those words. "And I'd have done the same thing all over again, Cristian, just to see you all suffer the way I did. And if Diego dies, you fucking deserve it. You deserve to have more blood on your hands, you sonofabitch!"

"No!" I jam the fork into his throat, digging it in as deep as it will go and dragging it down the front of his chest with every sliver of strength left in me. Blood gushes from his lips as his body convulses, his one eye on mine, wide open and filled with panic and fear.

That's what *he* deserves.

I grab the gun Tali dropped and plug him with bullets until his eye droops closed.

Evil bastard.

Rest in hell.

Heavy footsteps come barreling down the hall, and I run over to the doorway, crouched low and ready to shoot up any unwanted guests. Alek is right behind me.

It's good to know he has my back, especially after seeing what he can do with a fork.

Kaz and Leo appear with the Doc in tow.

"Everything still clear out there?" Alek asks.

They nod. "Yeah, but who knows for how long? There may be more on their way, so we need to make this fast," Kaz says, looking at Diego. "How is he?"

I grit my teeth. "How do you think?"

Doc glowers at Kaz. "While I work, why don't you make yourself useful and keep an eye out to make sure the rest of the place doesn't get shot up?"

Kaz grimaces but backs away, grabbing a stray gun.

The whole place looks like a messy arsenal right now with all of the guns scattered on the floor. An army of thugs, and none left standing.

Pretty fucking impressive.

The French have nothing on us.

Doc stands over Diego who has just started to stir and looks at me. "Let's get him on the bed. I need to get to work immediately to see what kind of damage was done."

Alek and I lift him off the floor and lay him in the center of the mattress. He lets out a weak groan. Hope clutches my heart.

That has to be a good sign, right?

My eyes flicker over to the Doc's, but he gives no indication either way. He looks at me, a grave expression on his face. I don't like that look. I push back my hair and pace as Doc opens one of his duffel bags and sets up his equipment. Tali and Alek back out of the room to give us privacy and I watch as Doc examines the wound and the surrounding area.

"He's so pale and cold," I mutter.

"He's in shock," Doc answers. "His oxygen levels have dropped, and his circulatory system is short-circuiting, which is why he looks and feels the way he does."

"Is he gonna die, Doc?" My voice rises, panic gripping me. "You can't let that happen. Please. Tell me what I need to do and I'll do it. Let's get him to the hospital, fly in specialists, whomever we need! Just don't....just don't let him go."

"Mnphh," Diego grunts, his eyelids opening a crack. "You sound pretty panicked, bro," he says in a thick, groggy voice.

I kneel down next to him, letting out a shaky breath. "Jesus, Diego. You scared the shit out of me."

"I didn't know you cared that much." He moans. "Christ, that hurts! What the hell happened?"

"It was that asshole, Jak Scala. Fucking guy turned on us." I narrow my eyes. "So I stabbed him with a fork."

Doc smirks. "I guess that's a lesson to me, huh?"

"Yeah," I mumble. "Screw with me or my family and you get filleted with eating utensils."

"Noted," Doc responds.

Diego's lips curl upward. "Never trust a guy who wears white socks and black shoes," he grumbles. I peek at Jak's feet. Sure enough, I catch a glimpse of white under his jeans.

I shake my head, chuckling. "At least your sense of humor didn't drain with half your blood supply."

Doc peers at the wound, cleaning the area and doing an examination of the entry point. "Okay, Diego. You're damn lucky this was a superficial wound. I just dressed it. Luckily, Jak managed to miss everything important. And your brother applied just the right amount of pressure while he waited for me. We'll need to get you to the hospital, but you're gonna pull through."

"Thank God," I groan, covering my face with my hand. Then I look at Diego. "How the hell did you manage to get beaten so badly in the first place? Jesus, didn't you learn anything I taught you?"

"Maybe you're just not that great of an instructor," he snips.

"Maybe you should just stick to women."

He lets out a weak snicker. "Some of the women I've been with are more violent than these assholes. You have no idea the kind of masochistic shit I've been through."

I shake my head. "You're sick."

"Yeah." He winks at me. "Shocker, right?"

Tali and Alek knock at the door, and I wave them in. "Looks like he's gonna make it after all."

"Thank God!" Tali exclaims, throwing her arms around me. "I'm so sorry about all of this," she murmurs in my ear. "Things could have gone so badly—"

I put a finger over her lips. "Stop. It's over. Leclercq is dead and so is his plan to take over our shipping business. You don't have to worry about him ever again."

"Don't I, though?" She looks up at me, her forehead lined with worry. "Those people, Daniel Tava's enemies. They're still coming, Cristian. They want what they're owed, and if we're the ones who are taking over his half of the company, they're going to find us and make sure they take everything."

"And if they do, we'll be ready for them." I tuck a strand of hair behind her ear, grazing her bruised face with my thumb and forefinger. "Nobody is going to hurt you. I won't let it happen."

She bites her lower lip, her eyes darting over to where Diego is bitching about his favorite shirt being ruined by the knifing. My face relaxes into a smile, and I pull her close. "Stop. I can tell you're nervous, but there's no reason to be."

"Are you sure? If I put any of us in danger...any of you in danger..." She shakes her head, her voice trailing off.

"You didn't do anything. And for the record, I'm still crazy about you," I murmur, a smile tugging at my lips.

Her eyes light up, her lips curling into a smile. One of those real ones that looks hopeful.

God, I'd wanted so badly to put one of those on her beautiful face since that night on the beach. And there it is, a sight I've waited for, one I was afraid I might not see again.

"You are?" she whispers.

"Yeah," I say, leaning my forehead against hers. "I love you, Tali."

"I love you, too," she says, her voice trembling and tears pooling in her eyes.

"So that's why you have to believe me, okay? I will never let anyone hurt someone I love. Besides, I've seen what your brother Alek can do with a fork. He's pretty damn resourceful."

Alek claps me on the back. "You didn't do too badly yourself."

"Yeah, well, I wasn't about to let you one-up me."

Alek nods. "Should make for an interesting partnership, don't you think?"

I smirk. "Who the hell would have guessed it in a million years, huh?"

"Partners, huh?" Diego says.

I lace my fingers with Tali's and bring them to my lips. "Yeah, until death."

Alek cocks an eyebrow. "And *whose* death still remains to be seen."

EPILOGUE

Tali

I walk outside onto the veranda of the Marcone home, leaning over the balcony and breathing in the fresh scent of basil and peaches as the late afternoon sun streams through the thick foliage.

It's so fragrant, and the sweet smells make my mouth water.

Of course, I can't imagine how I'd be hungry at all since I've done nothing but gorge myself on bread, olive oil, and cheese since we arrived in Sicily a week ago for a much-needed break.

It's also the first time Alek and I are meeting Cristian's family, something they planned since we're now all united under the shipping company that they now co-own.

Diego decided to return to Sicily permanently now that his dad's murder has been avenged. Finding out that Jak Scala was the one who put the hit on Joseph Marcone was a harsh pill for the family to swallow, but at least now they have the answers they'd been searching for. And although they're still struggling with the loss, their bond has become that much stronger.

I run a hand over my belly and swallow a groan. Cristian may just have to roll me onto the plane when we head back to Monaco in a few days. And he might need to buy me a second seat since I don't think I'll fit in the one we booked.

Even in first class.

I trace my finger over the stone railing, watching the sunlight glitter on the surface of deep blue lake below. Such a beautiful and peaceful countryside. It's hard to believe so many dangerous people occupy and unleash inexplicable havoc in such a pristine and perfect place.

It's equally impossible to believe that people here have such deep-rooted anger when there is so much deliciousness and decadence surrounding them on a daily basis.

Like prosciutto. And capicola. And soppressata. And parmesan.

Mmm...the list goes on and on.

But that's Sicily.

Costa Nostra.

With a backstory that's rich with crime, terror...

And cannoli.

I lick my lips, wondering what we'll be having for dinner.

Footsteps click on the stone patio, and then Cristian's strong arms wind around my waist, hugging me tight.

I groan. "Oh my God, I ate so much for lunch today. I think the button on my jeans is about to pop open."

He lets out a mischievous laugh. "How could that be bad? Anything that gets your pants off faster makes me very happy," he murmurs against my ear.

I let out a deep and contented sigh and turn to face him. "Would you still love me if I gained five-hundred pounds? Because if we ever relocate here, that may happen. I'm just letting you know that now."

He drops a kiss on the tip of my nose. "I'd love you if you gained five-thousand pounds."

"Aww, that's sweet."

"It's the truth."

"Hey, guys!" A sweet, feminine voice drifts out onto the patio just before Cristian's sister Gianna appears holding a bottle of wine and a tray of glasses. "Happy hour?"

I grin. "Sounds great! Do we have any cheese to pair with that wine?"

Cristian snicker-snorts, but I poke him in the side. "Don't even. You just told me you wouldn't care if I looked like an apartment building."

Gianna places the tray on a table and uncorks the wine. I can practically taste the rich flavors of the deep ruby liquid.

This place is seriously heaven on Earth.

"You are gorgeous, Tali. And your clothes look just as stunning on you today as they did when you flew in."

"Thanks." I take the glass with a smile. "You're an angel."

Gianna smiles. "I'm going to miss you guys when you leave."

"Well, you'll just have to come up to Monaco to visit us!"

"I would love that. But my brothers," she says, rolling her eyes. "They need me. God only knows what they'd do to this place if I was gone."

"You can't take care of them for your whole life," I say. "You need to take care of yourself, too."

"I know," Gianna says, sipping her wine. "I just...it's so hard, especially with Dad gone." She sighs. "We lost Mom so long ago and I made things easy on all of them by running this place. I filled her shoes and the boys got used to being taken care of." She grins at her brother. "Cristian and Diego were just as high maintenance before they took off for Monaco as Tommy, Vince, and Anthony are now."

"Oh yeah, well, guess what, baby sister? I'm back for good!" Diego snickers, coming outside and helping himself to a glass of wine.

Gianna groans. "Great." He snakes an arm around her waist and gives her a squeeze. "You know how much I love your meatballs. Nobody makes them better than you. How could I stay away a second longer?"

"How did I get so lucky?" Gianna moans, a playful smile on her face.

I love the banter between Cristian and his siblings. They really love each other and it's evident in the way they tease and torment each other. It makes me a little sad, truth be told. I really miss Kaz and Leo. And Alek...

He steps onto the veranda, his brows furrowed. Lately, he's been distracted. Abrupt. And a little more of a prick than he normally is.

I can't figure out why, and he shuts down every time I ask.

He and Cristian have spent a lot of time together since we arrived, meeting with clients and going through strategies and plans for the shipping company. I've asked Cristian about it, but he hasn't noticed anything off with Alek.

Sigh.

Men.

So unobservant.

I glance over at Gianna, who is still standing next to the table when Alek walks over. She looks up at him and narrows her eyes, her jaw set. He takes a sip of his wine and glares back at her before stalking over to the balcony.

What in the hell?

I breathe in the chianti in my glass and take a long sip. "Oh, that is *so* good," I moan.

"Hey, how come you don't moan this much when I'm fucking you?" Cristian whispers, nuzzling my neck. "I'm starting to get a complex."

I grab a cube of parmesan cheese from the tray and pop it into my mouth. "Oh, good Lord…"

"Okay, seriously. It's making me start to really question myself."

I giggle and pick up another cube of cheese when my stomach clenches so tight and causes such a sharp and excruciating pain, I actually gasp.

Then gag.

I clap a hand over my mouth and push past everyone.

The gagging is so violent and comes out of nowhere. I push open the door to the bathroom and collapse in front of the toilet, clutching the sides of the seat. Tears spring to my eyes. Oh God, the cheese must be bad. Holy crap.

The heaving continues for a few more seconds, and then all holy hell breaks loose. My stomach revolts against me and against all of the pasta, bread, and—

Argh! I can't even think about it!

"Tali," Cristian barges in, kneeling next to me and stroking the back of my head as the contents of my stomach reappear in front of my eyes.

I stay with my head in the toilet for a few minutes, struggling for breath after that horrific stomach explosion. It completely sapped me of all energy. I don't even think I can get off the floor if I tried. "I want to die." I moan.

"Are you just overdosed on cheese?" he asks with a smile, tracing a finger down the side of my cheek. "Maybe you need some water. Or tea? Maybe not ten desserts?"

"Uhhhh," I clutch my stomach again. "Shut up! You're such a jerk!"

He snickers. "I'm just teasing. But what happened? You've been fine for the whole trip. Maybe lunch didn't agree with you?" He leans close and hugs me to him. I bury my head in his neck and breathe in.

It's my very favorite cologne of his.

I smell cardamom, sage, bergamot...

My stomach clenches again and I yelp, pulling away and returning my head back to the toilet for the foreseeable future.

I collapse onto the floor after that second episode.

"God, what the hell is wrong with me? Is it still flu season?"

"I don't think so, but it could be a bug."

"I hope it's the twenty-four-hour kind," I mutter, rubbing my belly. It feels so bloated. Maybe I'm getting my period, not that puking my guts up is a symptom of PMS for me.

My heart damn-near stops.

Holy shit.

My period.

It's been eight weeks since we got together.

Eight weeks since we first had sex.

Without a condom.

And the pill is only ninety-nine-point-nine percent effective.

"Cristian," I rasp. "I don't think this bug is the twenty-four-hour kind. I think it might be more like the nine-month, eighteen-year kind."

IF YOU THOUGHT TALI AND CRISTIAN WERE HOT, IT'S NOTHING COMPARED TO THE FIRE BETWEEN ALEK AND GIANNA IN RAVAGE, A STEAMY AND FORBIDDEN AGE GAP MAFIA ROMANCE!

CLICK HERE TO READ RAVAGE—>

SNEAK PEEK OF RAVAGE

CHAPTER ONE: ALEK, SIX MONTHS AGO

I creep toward the hushed voices coming from the shore of the large lake. Moonlight reflects along the top of the rippling water as Carlo Santini skims rocks, trying to get each one to jump farther than the last.

But he sucks, so they just sink.

I narrow my eyes at the petite, dark-haired figure to his right. Gianna Marcone.

My brother-in-law Cristian's sister.

Even in the darkness, I can see her smile.

Christ, it can light up the sky.

At least in my mind it does.

I crouch down, palming the knife in the waistband of my jeans. I pull it out and click to pop it open, staring at the glimmering steel.

The perfectly sharpened tip.

The tip I'm going to use to stab Carlo Santini in the fucking eye if he does what I think he's about to do.

I grit my teeth as he turns toward her, dropping the remaining rocks in his hand.

He'd better watch that fucking hand…or he's gonna lose it.

A frustrated sigh escapes my mouth.

She shouldn't be here.

Nobody knows she sneaked out of the house and ran half a mile to Carlo's car because everyone in her life keeps her so sheltered that if she has to pee, they all escort her to the fucking bathroom to make sure she gets there okay.

It's only a little bit of an exaggeration.

She wants to rebel. I get it. She's been stifled for years, ever since Cristian saved her life from some crackpot bitch with a vendetta.

But she makes pretty fucking bad choices.

Case in point, Carlo.

Yeah, I know plenty about that blowhole.

I never walk into situations blind.

Not anymore.

I have eyes and ears everywhere.

I watch. I learn. I listen.

And only then do I act.

It's taken me a long time to get it right, and I've lost a lot in the process.

I didn't come to Sicily expecting that this woman would awaken things inside of me that I thought had died years ago. Ten years ago, to be exact.

I figured my heart was permanently out of commission, and I liked that. It's kept things simple for me. No romantic entanglements, no drama, no distractions.

That's all buried in my very sordid past.

Emotion just makes you weak, and in my business, weakness gets you killed.

Period.

And so now, here I am.

Because she's in real danger.

What's worse is she doesn't even suspect it.

She thinks Carlo is safe, that just because they've known each other for practically a lifetime, he'd never hurt her. She thinks he's one of the good guys.

Wrong, wrong, wrong!

Money talks, and my friend Carlo has gotten his pockets lined with plenty of cash to make this little rendezvous happen.

I narrow my eyes at Carlo. "Don't even fucking think about laying a finger on her, you bastard," I mutter, slowly rising to my feet.

They are only about fifty feet away, but I can't make out their words. Body language speaks plenty, though. As he pulls her close, my chest tightens. When she dips her head back, the hairs on the back of my neck prickle. And as her eyes drift closed, I silently spew expletives that would make a nun's ears bleed.

A rustling from my right side jolts me back to reality. I turn my head, narrowing my eyes in the darkness. There are plenty of thick bushes surrounding the area, but wind is at a minimum tonight.

Sounds are amplified in the darkness.

We have company.

I take a few deep breaths to calm my racing pulse as Carlo's hands travel the slope of Gianna's spine. Her back arches, her hips thrusting forward as he fists her long dark hair.

Motherfucker!

I grip the knife tight in my hand, imagining how good it's gonna feel when I slam the blade right into his fucking carotid artery.

More rustling comes from a nearby bush.

The lovebirds don't notice anything, but I do.

And I don't like it.

Seconds seem to stretch into hours as I wait, hunched over in my own bush.

She didn't know what she was walking into tonight, but I did.

I always know.

But I didn't say a word to anyone because I wanted to be the one to save her from Carlo.

I just didn't count on an audience. And I'm damn curious to see who's about to join the party. Luckily, I don't have long to wait because while Carlo has his tongue stuck down Gianna's throat, three big guys jump out of the bushes.

Short and stocky, they're wearing jeans, t-shirts, and Nikes.

They'd be best advised to fucking run their assess off now while they have the chance.

I can hear Gianna gasp from my spot in the darkness. Carlo flashes an evil smirk at her and waves the guys over. I drop my knife in the grass and pull out my gun.

I always carry multiple weapons because you just never know.

And since I'm not one to count on anyone coming to *my* rescue, I need the added insurance.

Thank fuck I've had an eye on Carlo since I landed here in Sicily a couple of weeks ago.

I'm not proud to admit I've had my eye on Gianna, too.

I've watched her when I thought nobody was looking...the way her hair falls over her shoulders in loose waves, the way her dark eyes twinkle when she laughs, the red ring that appears on her lips after she's had one glass too many of the famous chianti her family makes. God, I want to suck off every last drop.

And that's when I really love to fantasize about that body plastered over mine, her hot mouth wrapped tight around my dick, her tan, toned legs straddling me...

But I wasn't as careful as I thought because someone else picked up on the longing stares.

Cristian.

He only made a few passing comments to start, but there were always thinly veiled threats weaved into his words.

Until he flat out told me to stay the hell away from his sister.

It pisses me off that I showed my hand. I never do.

But Gianna...God, she has an effect on me, like nothing I've ever experienced.

Makes me want to take my chances with her ridiculously overprotective brother.

But I know it can never happen. *We* can never happen, for so many reasons.

And that's why I need to come up with some excuse for being here tonight...something that doesn't make me look like a complete fucking stalker. Which could be difficult because that's basically what I am.

Tonight isn't the first night she's escaped from her house, which I know because I've been watching. Closely. But it is the first time she's in danger of never going back.

The Sicilian mafia doesn't forget things like debts that are owed, even if the guy who owes them is dead as a fucking doornail.

They find other ways to collect.

I cock my gun and point it at the three beefy jackasses, expelling a frustrated sigh. I know they won't kill her.

Not yet, anyway.

They need her as leverage for their boss.

The one who wants to collect.

And if there's one thing the Marcone family will bend over for, it's Gianna.

But I don't trust that these guys will give her up that easily, even if they get their damn money. And I know they'll come after the shipping business that Cristian and I co-own next because these seedy cockroaches just infiltrate every fucking thing.

They take it all and still come back for more.

I swallow hard as Carlo twists Gianna around, his arm tight around hers. Her squeals of pain echo in the still air. "Carlo, get the hell off of me! What are you doing?"

The other three idiots leer at her and one has the nerve to run his hand down the front of her shirt.

Fucker. I'm gonna kill you first.

Carlo leans close and whispers something I can't make out. Adrenaline courses through my veins as Gianna's cries get louder.

Not that it matters. We're not in a place where anyone can hear her.

Or witness what I'm about to do to the men whose hands are now all over her.

I should call Cristian. This is his family's fight. I'm just an unlucky associate.

But I don't want her family to know that I've been watching her every move.

Because it's only partially out of concern.

Mostly, it's because I'm crazy about her. It's a fact I've tried to keep hidden for weeks because she's Cristian's sister and because being with me is never in anyone's best interest.

Like Lina's.

That's why I keep myself closed off, why I don't trust people, why I won't let them get close. I can't take unnecessary risks or people I love will die.

And Cristian knows it.

He's seen what I'm capable of, and the qualities he likes in me as his business partner are not the ones he wants in a guy who lusts after his sister.

I narrow my eyes as Gianna's expression morphs into one of terror. I'm guessing that right about now, Carlo has told her that she's never going to see her family again.

Goddammit!

Why the fuck did she need to sneak away? Why did she allow herself to be sucked in by *him*, of all the greasy, pizza-eating, wine-guzzling motherfuckers here in Sicily? Why does she need to be so fucking rebellious?

Why, why, why?

I'm going to have a lot to explain to my new partner.

Later.

I can't sit here with my thumb up my ass, concocting a story.

Right now, I need to make sure there's a story to tell...one with a satisfying ending.

I squeeze my eyes shut. But I don't say a prayer.

I never do.

Don't need to.

I leap out of the bushes and run toward the group. Time slows to the point where it almost stops, and I leap at Carlo's dipshit pals first, shocking them so that I can take the first shots. Even in the darkness, I never miss my mark.

Crack! Pop! Bang!

Two of them crumble to the ground in a heap, but the third guy, he's scrappy. He manages to escape my bullets and rolls away from me so he can grab his own gun. The guy takes a few shots while he looks for cover…shots I easily avoid.

Game on, motherfucker.

There's nothing that's gonna keep me from blowing off your head.

Gianna's whimpers make my throat tight, and I know before I even look that Carlo has a gun pointed at her head and his arm wrapped around her chest, shielding him. I can tell what a fucking coward is gonna do before he does it.

Only when Carlo's last peon turns his panicked eyes at me do I know for sure he's finished.

His clip is now empty, and I'm still alive, all because he's a suck-ass shot. I point my gun at him and squeeze off a couple of shots.

Pop! Pop!

He lands on the ground with a satisfying thud. I'm not even out of breath when I turn toward Carlo. He looks like he's about to shit himself, if he hasn't already.

The corners of my lips curl into a smirk. "I'm gonna go out on a limb here and say that you know I'm not here to settle your boss' debt."

Tears stream down Gianna's face, her lips quivering.

All I want is to wrap my arms around her and bury my head in her sweet-smelling neck.

But that's something I'll never get to do.

Instead, I'll be her savior. At least for tonight.

"I'm a big fan of messages, Carlo." I take a few steps toward him, slowly. His eyes are wide with fear, but he doesn't speak. I cock my head. "Seems like you were saying a lot to Gianna before. Now you've got nothing? I'm surprised. I'd heard you were some big bad ginzo gangster. I'm a little disappointed." I shake my head, circling them. He turns and twists around, never taking his eyes off of me.

"I don't know who you are, but I'll fucking kill her! Her family needs to pay, and if you're smart, you'll take that message back to them."

"I could do that," I say, pretending to think about that half-ass threat. "Or I could kill you, find your family, kill them, and then go and have a glass of wine back at the house. With Gianna and her family."

"Fuck you, asshole! You won't get off one shot!" He cocks his gun and Gianna lets out a shriek, clawing at his arms. "It's my way or she fucking dies!"

I smirk. "Nah, not tonight. I like my way better." I point my gun at Carlo and shoot once, hitting him right between the eyes. A thin stream of blood drizzles from where the bullet lodged itself and his arms go slack right before he falls backward into the shallow lake water.

I eliminate threats.

It's what I do best.

Gianna rushes into my arms, nestling her tear-streaked face against my chest, sobs shuddering her body. I allow myself a single minute to stroke her soft hair, to feel her heartbeat thump in time with my own, and to become intoxicated by her fresh floral scent.

It's bliss.

And at the same time, it's the worst kind of torture.

Because I know it will be the closest I will ever be to her again.

Keep Reading Ravage —>

MEET KRISTEN

Kristen Luciani is a *USA Today* bestselling author of steamy and suspense-filled romance. She's addicted to kickboxing, Starburst jelly beans, and swooning over dark, broken anti-heroes. Kristen is happily married to her own real-life hero of over 20 years.

In addition to penning spicy stories, she also has a part-time job as her three kids' personal Uber driver, which she manages to successfully juggle along with her other tasks: laundry, cleaning, laundry, cooking, laundry, and caring for her adorable Boston Terrier puppy. Mafia romance is her passion...and her poison.

Join Me On Patreon
https://www.patreon.com/kristenluciani

Follow for Giveaways

FACEBOOK KRISTEN LUCIANI - http://on.fb.me/1Y87KjV

Private Reader Group
THE STILETTO CLICK - http://bit.ly/2iQBr5V

VIP Newsletter
CLICK HERE TO JOIN MY VIP NEWSLETTER - https://dl.bookfunnel.com/28e0amc80q

Feedback Or Suggestions For New Books?
Email Me! KRISTEN@KRISTENLUCIANI.COM

Want To Join My ARC Team?
JOIN MY AMAZING ARC TEAM! - https://www.facebook.com/groups/316777206096987

Want A FREE Book?
CLICK HERE TO DOWNLOAD! - https://bit.ly/2Jubp8h

Instagram
@KRISTEN_LUCIANI

BookBub
FOLLOW ME ON BOOKBUB - https://bit.ly/2FIcoP1

- facebook.com/kristenlucianiauthor
- x.com/kristen_luciani
- instagram.com/kristen_luciani

Made in the USA
Middletown, DE
12 July 2024

57150432R00156